HIDEOUS EXUBERANCE

Stephen C. Bird

A previous version of "Hideous Exuberance" was registered with the Library of Congress on September 25th, 2009.

All images and photographs
© 2009, 2011 and 2012 by Stephen C. Bird

Cover design by Stephen C. Bird

ISBN-10: 0615581706
ISBN-13: 9780615581705

Dedicated to

My Family, My Friends, My Colleagues, My Associates, My Supporters, My Detractors, My Idols, My Nemeses and The Universe ……….

TABLE OF CONTENTS

1	Szczmawgwhore(ts): A Pornographick Bitch-Story	1
2	Glowing Green Gas	35
3	Gondolphus Clownhouse	47
4	Djzheemi Sparks	63
5	The Travails of Ginger Bocey	81
6	Francine Kafka	105
7	Bobby Chushingura	117
8	The Revenge of Alison Sh*tbox	127
9	Volodya Gufo y La Familia	137
10	Gothra Schvulkopf and The Daily Grind	157
11	Gothra Schvulkopf and Her Pumpkin Trolls	179
12	The Preiszcz is Wright	197

SZCZMAWGWHORE(ts): A PORNOGRAPHICK BITCH-STORY

SZCZMAWGWHORE(TS): A PORNOGRAPHICK BITCH-STORY

Higher Parterre and his best friend Traan Mrs. Beasley took a break from the stacks of homework heaped upon them by Professor MacGagitall and settled in for a game of Hoorny Boore, a hypothetickal deconstrucktion of their friend Whoremoania Gangster's future life in pornographie. Whoremoania was the daughter of Szczmoogle-Bjzhorgs with scaly, chameleonick skin – a race that suppressed awareness of uncomfortable realities and submitted to brainwashing by the Krystal Lite Side, the Force for Good in the province of Galeeszczya – in the Whorey Roboman Empire where our story takes place. Malfaux, the former enemy of Higher, Traan and Whoremoania in their days as children with good prospeckts, had brought them over to the Not-So-Krystal Lite Side, courtesie of a Pseudo-Druidyck spell that he had run across while trespassing in the Retarded Secktion of the Szczmawgwhorets library (or the "Mentally Challenged" Secktion as it was known to the politickally-correckt, peer-pressure influenced students of Szczmawgwhorets). Szczmawgwhorets was an institution for sorcerers-in-training located in the highlands of Galeeszczya. Higher, Traan and Whoremoania were known around school as *The Unholie Trynytie*. All three of them were now fifteen years old and deep in the clutches of pubertie-inspired confusion.

Against the wishes of their former supporters from the Krystal Light Side, *The Unholie Trynytie* had transferred from the reputable house of Gryffynwhore to despicable Sliturine [Gryffynwhore, Sliturine, Reganbarf and Puffynstuff constituted the four houses of Szczmawgwhorets]. In accordance with his Faustian bargain with Malfaux, Higher was teaching Dharma-Puta Tongue, the Komodo Dragon Speech of Quasibjzhorg [the Anti-Szczmoogle Bjzhorg, commonly known as *He Who Would Not Be Loved*] to the students of Szczmawgwhorets. Higher was also stitching together prom dresses fashioned from the lavender tapestries of the Sliturine common room – a house known for its delinquent, yet effeminate, population. Higher had already made peace with his feminine side in a way that was highly evolved for a presumably straight teenage boy. *The Unholie Trynytie* and Malfaux thumbed their noses in disrespeckt at Kallous Humblewhore, Head Neckro-Misère of Szczmawgwhorets, choosing to embrace instead the four witches from the popular Amurycka Profundan film, *The Kräft*, as their supernatural guides.

The Bjzhorgermeister of Maniackally Obsessive-Compulsive Eradickation, Antithesis Reticence, encouraged abstinence in all of the students of Szczmawgwhorets – to render them less vulnerable to *He Who Would Not Be Loved*. Although authentick pornographie was hard to come by at Szczmawgwhorets, hypocritickal Evilangelists from Amurycka Profunda were willing to smuggle in pornographick DVDs to interested students – for a price. And even then, the qualitie of the pornographie was uneven. The Evilangelists knew that they could take advantage of naïve students – and so instead of authentick pornographie – the students received films starring various unknown soft-core pornographick acktors employed by Lifetime, the Women's Channel.

Professor Frivolous Snide, one of Quasibjzhorg's double agents, had always despised Higher Parterre for his special powers and he had now come to fear those powers as well. Higher was the son of two renowned and deceased Krystal Light Side sorcerers; Quasibjzhorg, in trying to destroy Higher, who had been reputed to be the Second Coming of Hey-Zeus-I-Juana Morafin, had acktually made Higher more powerful. Snide was sadistick and was fully aware that risks were involved in the teaching of his field [Occultyck Occupations]. In instructing his students to defend themselves against Quasibjzhorg and his Minions of Morewhore [Morewhore was a dark, smoky, volcanick land full of steaming rivers, toxic toys and human rights abuses] – Snide had intentionally ended several of those students' lives, denying all responsibilitie by claiming their deaths as accidents. Snide's powers had their origins in the Abyss of the Dollblog [an ancient fiery demon residing in the icy depths of the Bottomless Pit of Middl Earf Hampton. The Dollblog had taught Snide the infamous Hemorrhoidal Halitosis potions that involved the switching places of the mouth and the ass]. As revenge for those outrageous murders, Higher had cast a spell on Snide – the irrevocable Grassy Ass charm – causing matte-gray-black stars, sparks and smoke to pour from the professor's ears, eyes, nose, mouth and asshole – whenever Higher deemed necessary. Snide had recently caught Higher roaming the halls of the upper floors of Szczmawgwhorets after curfew and threatened to report him to Kallous Humblewhore. But Higher coolly warned Snide ..... "You wouldn't dare. Malfaux has in his possession photographick evidence of your latest oral servicing of Goldie-Boy Foockhart [Szczmawgwhoret's Homo Eckonomickus professor]. Everything cuts both ways Snide – and your job is certainly more important than my innockuous delinquencie, *n'est-ce pas?* So – are you ready for more ill-humoured matte-gray-black stars, sparks, and smoke to invade your corporeal being – *Ye Who Thinkest That Thou Knowest Everything?*"

PONDERING THE FUTURE

Basking in the glow of the Sliturine common room fire, *The Unholie Trynytie* dreamt of their future careers. Traan Mrs. Beasley, after becoming a billionaire selling bottles of Lyckwyd Narnya to an uninformed publick, would then become the Ambassador to Morewhore and negotiate contrackts between Blorks, Bjzhorks, Sin-Torrids, Hoollywood Moomies, Multi-Specktral Neckro-Tanzers and all the rest of the unquestionably loyal followers of *He Who Would Not Be Loved*. Malfaux wanted to learn the ways of the hypocritickal Evilangelists and move up in the ranks of I-PORN-DEE-NET [the International Pornographick Distribution Network]. Higher envisioned himself as a ruthless C-E-I-E-O, dedicated to the environmental rape of Third World Szczmoogle-Bjzhorg lands. Whoremoania, Szczmawgwhorets' fallen angel, dreamt of her first starring role in a bestiality film, *Barebacked by Foockbeeck* [Foockbeeck was a Lipo-Creep – an archetypal creature resembling a saber-toothed dodo bird-hippopotamus with pterodacktyl wings, bear claws, an elephant's trunk – and a tiara from the 99 Cent Store on West 14th Street between 6th and 7th Avenues. Nueva Jork].

Whoremoania had seen her future more clearly than her less mature cohorts and that future lay in pornographick films. A road less traveled by young ladies from respeckabibble Szczmoogle-Bjzhorg families – nonetheless a road that was easy to navigate once the burdensome moralitie with which such girls had been raised had been jettisoned. Whoremoania, ahead of her oafish male peers erotickally as well as intellecktually, had just finished reading Arthur Miller's *The Crucible* and sought to re-create the dynamicks of the relationship between protagonist John Procktor and antagonist Abigail Williams – in all of her affairs ..... she drifted off into a reverie .....

Imagine ..... the only way those 17th centurie Puritan Amurycka Profundans could have any fun was to break the rules of their own stiflingly rigid culture. Once again, I am confronted with the double-edged specktre of heretickal blasphemie. I will cast an Erecktokankersaurus spell upon Goldie Boy Foockhart and lead him into the savage anarchie of my Bower of Bliss! Even if it turns out that he is a Pro-Fag-Onanyst, his body will respond to my desire ….. Whoremoania had started speaking softly to herself in a back-in-the-day Nueva Jork bag lady kind of way. She had developed a romantick obsession with her favorite professor, Goldie-Boy Foockhart, and was determined to arrange a clandestine meeting with him in the South Tower of Gryffynwhore [her former house] ….. *Without special permission from Professor Mac-Gagitall, and especially at night, I am forbidden to step on the premises of Gryffynwhore. But to the South Tower of Gryffynwhore in the night I will go. I will set a trap for Goldie-Boy Foockhart. I have learned all of the necessary charms. Sexual transgression elevates erotick intensitie ….. she whispered to herself between* classes, licking her lips in greedy anticipation. Whoremoania and Goldie-Boy Foockhart met soon thereafter and commenced their secret love affair.

ESTEBAN GRIMGORIO

Like most of Galeeszczya's Anglophone population, Higher and Traan struggled with Spanish in Donya Contra Madrugadora's class. When Donya

SZCZMAWGWHORE(TS): A PORNOGRAPHICK BITCH-STORY

Contra Madrugadora inquired of the class ..... *¿Habla todavía Jorge Booszcz español?* ..... the students responded in unison ..... *No, el no habla ni español, ni inglés* ..... Because they were not dekooning-linguistickally gifted, Higher and Traan had taken on Esteban Grimgorio, Szczmawgwhorets' Meso-Amuryckan exchange student, to do their Spanish homework. Esteban was an Azteck ocktoroon whose fair skin betrayed not the slightest hint of *mestizo* blood. Not only was he a Francophile, he also spoke Italian with a Sud Amurycka Profundan accent and had convinced everyone that he came from Buenas Heiress, Archie-Bettyna, Sud Amurycka Profunda. As for Frivolous Snide – yes he too loved all things French – including Esteban. Thus far in life Snide had never experienced carnal love that was not unrequited – perhaps because his inauthenticitie was comparable to that of a slumming New England aristocrat passing for the prep school gardener.

As for Malfaux – he had recently hurled a first year rising star of Puffynstuff, Goofie Bouffawhnt, to his death from a window at the top of the West Tower of Puffynstuff – a copycat murder inspired by the film

Braveheart. It had been agreed upon by all of the students of Puffynstuff that Goofie was the student "most likely to fall through the cracks"; therefore in disposing of Goofie, Malfaux was merely executing the desire of their collecktive will. And any Puffynstuffer who disagreed with Malfaux's acktions in this regard, became the vicktim of a brain enema spell – a simple incantation that went like this: EENEE-MEANY, EENEE-MINEY, EENEE-MAH! Snide used the occurrence of Goofie's murder as an excuse to exackt revenge on Malfaux. Snide cast a spell on Malfaux that caused maroon-brick-red-mauve-chocolate *molé* blood to flow permanently from Malfaux's asshole. So deep and dark was the execution of Snide's magick in this instance – that Malfaux would have to wear a male-ass-tampon for the rest of his sorcerer life.

Back in her private bedroom in Sliturine, Whoremoania lay on her back naked, ignoring her homework, caressing her breasts, legs in the air, pleasuring herself, phantasming about Punanie Pac-Manson and herself being double-date gang raped by Kallous Humblewhore and Promotheus Sludge [the Pink Brown Soothsayer and the Pseudo-Druidyck High

Priest of Sex and Shit]. Whoremoania resented most authoritie figures – but in her role-playing fantasie life – all hierarchies were inverted and she became powerless by design. The two other members of *The Unholie Trynytie* had recently hatched a plot against Whoremoania; Higher and Traan were envious of her, as they lacked her sexual sophistication. Shifting loyalties of this kind had become commonplace during Szczmawgwhoret's *Euripidean* decline. Higher and Traan had arranged for Whoremoania's sexual violation and impregnation with the demon seed of Quasibjzhorg. Higher and Traan cast a *Nottambulo* spell on Snide with the intention of using him as their zoombie spy for *He Who Would Not Be Loved*. In his zoombie spy state, Snide witnessed Whoremoania professing her love for Goldie-Boy Foockhart in the little-used powder room of the North Tower of Sliturine. Snide reported this information back to Higher and Traan, who then relayed it to Quasibjzhorg. Higher and Traan subsequently hypnotized Whoremoania and guided her to the Sliturine North Tower powder room ..... *He Who Would Not Be Loved* then appeared, metamorphosed himself into Goldie-Boy

Foockhart and proceeded to express his amorous desires for Whoremoania ..... Quasibjzhorg-as-Goldie-Boy had come to her in a dream à la *Rosemary's Baby*. Whoremoania was swept off her feet. Then *He Who Would Not Be Loved* had his way with her ..... leaving her traumatized and blubbering on the floor of the North Tower Sliturine powder room.

After her periods stopped, Whoremoania started to have nightmares that led her to realize that she had been raped by an evil spirit. In her panick, she searched for a suitable abortion-inducing potion in the Retarded ("Mentally Challenged") Secktion of the Szczmawgwhorets library. But the page in the Course-Curse Book that Whoremoania was looking for regarding the specific *Incantesimi Necessari* had been ripped out by Punanie Pac-Manson, the supposedly immackulate prefeckt of Puffynstuff who had skillfully concealed her own tarnished reputation. In a desperate effort to destroy her demon fetus, Whoremoania poured a bottle of amyl nitrate (that she had acquired via her trysts with Goldie Boy Foockhart) into a toilet bowl in the North Tower Sliturine powder room, lit a match and set the poppers-water on fire. She then sat her pink-brown asshole down over the flames. Her post-rape trauma has caused her to seek out ass-immolation as a form of ritual purifickation. The fetus was evackuated and before losing consciousness, Whoremoania managed to crawl to the office of Madame Pompino, the Big Nurse of Szczmawgwhorets. Madame Pompino promptly unpotted a baby *madrigauloise* (a creature that was half castrato, half ginseng root) straightaway, pointing its screaming face at Whoremoania's sphinckter. The *madrigauloise* was known for working wonders on maladies of the ass. Although the madrigauloise saved Whoremoania from permanent injurie, a rigorous rehabilitation awaited her. Every day for six months afterward, for one hour twice daily, Whoremoania soothed her barbecued buttocks in an aluminum washtub filled with chilled Vaseline. She eventually made a full recoverie, with the exception of unforeseen side effeckts of the scream of the madrigauloise. Huge collagen and botox enhanced lips, as well as oversized white buckteeth, appeared on either side of her ass crack. And her buttocks inflated to the size of basketballs. At first, Whoremoania was happy with her newly collagenated and botoxed *derrière*. But once she was fully healed, she decided otherwise – thus she started to create potions of transformation. For a time, just for fun, Whoremoania metamorphosed herself into a clone of that infamous Amurycka Profundan Park Avenue Nueva Jork socialite, Joker-Lynn Wildey-Thyme ..... Whoremoania knew that she had evolved beyond Amurycka Profundan culture. Yet she was hypocritickally enamoured of the way that its lingering Puritanism and pornographie encouraged shameful self-abasement, sexual self-hatred, lascivious low self-esteem and a gnawing need for surgickal reconstrucktion.

One morning, shortly after her recoverie was complete, Whoremoania made her debut as Sliturine's exhibitionist. Her dorm room door was open and her bare ass faced the hallway, as she read a well-worn paperback copy of *American Psycho* in doggy-style position. She had purposely soiled her gold *lamé* panties so that they would resemble those of a crack addickt hoostler from circa 1980s Times Square, Nueva Jork. A pile of dirty socks, jockstraps and thongs lay on her pillow, providing a unique bouquet of savory scents. She had found these items on E-Bay and they had been delivered to her via FedEx Parrot [Green-black parrots delivered all of the mail between Galeeszczya and the rest of the Blue Green Planet]. A shipment of Sud Amurycka Profundan green-black parrots had escaped in Galeeszczya twenty years before and thanks to global warming, the parrots had successfully adjusted to Galeeszczya's now subtropickal climate. Whoremoania's gold *lamé* panties functioned as a Porn-Key, enabling her to easily physio-animate between the pre-gentrified Times Square area of Eighth Avenue (between 42nd and 49th Streets) Nueva Jork and present-day Szczmawgwhorets ..... On winter nights in the luxurious anti-comfort of the Sliturine dormitorie, she lay wide awake, listening to the howling winds, watching serene snowfalls and stargazing when apropos. Whoremoania was awed by the beautie of winter at Szczmawgwhorets. However, she was unable to share this feeling with anyone, since warm and fuzzie sentiments of this kind were prohibited in Sliturine. If such feelings were ever psychickally divined by Szczlaawf, the Sliturine prefeckt, the offender would promptly receive the following punishment: mandatorie detention, obligatorie homework during vacations and the inabilitie to practice magick for an entire semester. Innocence battled with experience in her mind and she longed for the blissful unawareness of her non-magickal Szczmoogle-Bjzhorg childhood …..

….. *What had happened to this brilliant child who had spent all of those summers, designed for her cultural expansion, in France? She had let go of her aristockratick aspirations after her Szczmoogle-Bjzhorg parents were killed in a car crash en route from Avignon to Aix-en Provence ….. four years earlier during her 11th year. For better or for worse, Whoremoania was no longer tormented by the high moral standards with which she had been raised. At the same time, the French that she had learned was slipping away. To remedy this, she had started meeting with Esteban Grimgorio and Frivolous Snide at their extracurricular Salon des Fartistes ….. where Esteban and Snide laughed blatantly at Whoremoania's mediocre French pronunciation, like a pair of dueling Blanches du Bois des Boulognes. As a result of this abuse at the Salon des Fartistes, Whoremoania vowed to have her revenge, making the decision to let the evil flower within her bloom to its fullest.* She now embraced the lowest influences imported from the coarsening culture of Amurycka Profunda. She visualized her life at age 25. That life would be a double life ..... pornographick film star by night – chairwoman of the UCLA Department of Demonologie by night. She had decided that there would be no daytime in her future life ..... Only Night plus Night ..... "NIGHT + NIGHT = DOUBLE DARK = DOUBLE BLACK". That was the mantra that she chanted to herself during stressful Szczmawgwhortian moments .....

It was common knowledge that the Evilangelists of Amurycka Profunda purchased more pornographie than any other demographick of that nation. And it was the approval of that group that Whoremoania desired more than any other. In pursuit of this goal, Malfaux had helped her to establish contackts in the pornographick industrie and she had secretly started working as a model / esckort as well (although if anyone happened to ask her what she was doing with her life, she would tersely reply "I'm an acktress"). Intellecktual gifts not necessary for this career had been placed in a metallick, iridescent, Art New-Faux, *blue-within-blue* box. This box required two different types of *blue-within-blue* keys to open it ….. the first mid-20th centurie institutional, the second mid-19th centurie Pre-Raphaelite. This particular Art New-Faux *blue-within-blue* box was kept in a subterranean vault in Klyngon-Knots [a bank controlled by vicious Blorks from Morewhore] that was located in Die-Fag-Anon Alley, Szczmawgford-on–Avon-Laidie.

After Whoremoania had clandestinely made her first pornographick film, she took a reprieve and construckted a Wykkan Wykker Man bonfire in a mountain meadow above Szczmawgwhorets. She destroyed all of her books in this fire because she was so ashamed of who she was. She had convinced herself that she wanted to eradicate her brilliant mind and give herself over entirely to Quasi-bjzhorg ….. she started to ruminate ….. *It's my intelleckt that's stopping me from getting what I want in life. From now on, I will make split-second decisions not requiring the baggage of reflecktion or analysis* (she rationalized) ….. *bad grammar will be my passport to success* ….. Whoremoania's willingness to degrade herself had quickly brought her fame in the demi-monde of pornographie. She fell into a night dream under the hot lights during a break from filming *Unspeakable Karnal Travestie*. In her NIGHT + NIGHT dream ..... *she was escaping up the California coast north of Lost Angelist ..... wired like Busby Berkeley after a brutal day of megalomaniackal filming ..... wired like Frances Farmer hurling towards a run-in with the cops and the prelude to her dénouement ..... wired like Edie Sedgwick living in an empty swimming pool in the backyard of her mother's California mansion .....* Whoremoania was awakened by the sound of the fluffer and the direcktor having a violent argument. She rolled her eyes – already sex for pay had become so banal. She would just have to grin and bear it. She still had one more film to complete before she could take a vacation from sex. The plot of her latest film concerned a bisexual *ménage à trois* performed at a party – before an audience of deeply closeted Middle Eastern princes – who were on business in Vashink-Tone, the capital city of both the District of Amoebya and Amurycka Profunda as well.

HIDEOUS EXUBERANCE

As Whoremoania had done, Punanie Pac-Manson also dreamt of a life in pornographie. Unfortunately, having had detrimental spells cast upon her after having fallen out of favor with Frivolous Snide – Punanie's buckteeth now stuck out at a 90 degree angle. And where her breasts had formerly been, two feet now stuck out from her chest, enhanced by a violet eye on the bottom of each sole. A year later, Punanie Pac-Manson made a unickorn snuff film – that tragickally ended up being her first pornographick projekt ..... as well as her last .....

Whoremoania eventually quit the pornographie business and spent the rest of her leave of absence from Szczmawgwhorets writing, and then publishing, her first book entitled: *Reclaiming Lost Innocence: Lessons Learned From My Walks of Schäme*. By going publick with her issues, Whoremoania was able to let go of her rebellious phase and to begin building towards tangible success. She quickly reacclimated herself to the academick life of a sorceresse-in-training. On one stormy day, Traan Mrs. Beasley found Whoremoania sequestered in the Szczmawgwhorets librarie, where she was thinking out loud while using disposable lighters to make ashtrays out of second-hand vinyl reckords ..... "How can the paranormal sexiness of *The Kräft* be rightly compared to the utter wholesomeness of *Mistyckal Pizza Fäce?*" she queeried Traan ..... In spite of her recent conversion, the wheels of perversion were still turning in her mind. Whoremoania suggested a plan for the De-Fleuring of Higher Parterre to Traan. Whoremoania knew that Traan was jealous of Higher's ever-growing popularitie and so she goaded him on like a Shakespearian villainesse ..... *Traan – I want you to torture Higher by pretending to be gay-for-pay. I will transform Higher into a mindless sex zoombie who will be completely under my control. Then you can anally rape him while he rams my crootch with his Antagonystyck 7000 [a magickal mop used by Quispiszcz players – Quispiszcz was a sport played at Szczmawgwhorets in which students tried to burn each other with flaming mops – or Molotov Moptails as they were known in the colloquial] ..... Maybe Higher can Quispiszcz-fly – but can he poosey-fly? Or be he a faggy fag?*

Whoremoania felt constrickted by the confines of Szczmawgwhorets and its plethora of rules.

HIDEOUS EXUBERANCE

To compensate, she drifted into a Day Daze ….. Although I'd miss the margarine-beer of Szczmawgweed Tavern in Szczmawgford-on-Avon-Laidie, as well as the skillful pole-dancing technique of that tavern's bar wench, Pentacostya Koontwytch ….. I long to drive along the interior roads of Mayne, Amurycka Profunda ….. a land far inferior to Galeeszczya that will eventually fall under the control of Morewhore. The Mayne I want to experience is the one that enchanted Stephen Queen as a child and deepened his understanding of pure evil [like his forbear Nathan-Yell Whorethorne, Stephen Queen found inspiration in the 17th century ghosts of Amurycka Profunda.] Then I will head on down to Salem, Massachusetts, birthplace of pure evil. I will become intimately acquainted with its current demographick. Its WASPs and their heritage are dying off quickly – undoubtedly the area is now mostly Latino – thank Lord Szczmawg for that! I'll be able to get laid without experiencing any hangover of Puritan guilt! Then I will physio-animate to Mistyck, Kynetyck-Koont, the setting for my favorite PG-rated film ever ….. Mistyckal Pizza Fäce ….. a movie about

SZCZMAWGWHORE(TS): A PORNOGRAPHICK BITCH-STORY

three teenage girls who comfort and support each other while living through a dizzying roller coaster of adolescent phantasms. They learn hard lessons, they roll with the punches and they always get back on the horse! Oh – To live in a world of all things Szczmoogle-Bjzhorg! ..... Then Whoremoania returned to realitie ..... with all of its accompanying ugliness .....

Due to his special powers, only Higher Parterre managed to avoid Malfaux's hypnotick influence. Unbeknownst to Traan and Malfaux, Higher had split his soul into 7 Whorecrootches; in doing so, he gradually became overpowered by Quasibjzhorg. Higher's belated mother, Oxymoronycka Parterre, had died proteckting Higher from the mortal effeckts of the vituperous Iphana-Iphanka spell, cast upon Higher by *He Who Would Not Be Loved*. Oxymoronycka would never let Higher forget that she had sackrificed her life for him. She chastised Higher from Valhaha in his dreams, frequently offering him unsolicited advice in a heavy Galeeszczean brogue ..... "For Quasibjzhorg's sake – date the homecoming queen and get her to foockin bloo ya!" she spewed out at him unceremoniously .....

HIDEOUS EXUBERANCE

One morning, Penelope the Peloponnesian Parrot delivered a letter from Madame Saline to Higher. Madame Saline was the paramour of Fag-Greed, the Jolly Gigantyck Janytor of Szczmawgwhorets. Fag-Greed was starting to bore her and so Madame Saline had cast her eye upon Higher, as monogamie was incomprehensible to her (not to mention the fact that she was a chicken hawk as well) …..

Dear Higher,

Fag-Greed had his hands all over me last night. He took me to an obscure powder room on an upper-floor of the East Tower of Reganbarf, so that ghostly Molesting Me Molesta Myrna could watch us foock. He squeezed my breasts like he was cracking Lipo-Creep eggs! Very sensual this guy! (Am I making you uncomforbibble with my X-rated banter? I hope so!) Then he threw me down on my back. I raised my legs and readied myself for the beast. When he thrust his moonster coock deep inside me ….. I thought I was going to expire. 15 minutes later ….. la petite mort est arrivé ….. êtes-vous jaloux, Higher?

I'm all alone here, Higher. I'm on my back now, legs up in the air, gripping my ankles, rocking back and forth. I'm very hot and very wet. But it's not Fag-Greed that I want this time. He's busy being responsabibble and respeckabibble – YAWN! IT'S YOU THAT I WANT HIGHER – I'M WAITING FOR YOU! Anyways ….. Fag-Greed is AC/DC. He's probably out being molested by a Vladivostokian Vlad-Impala as we speak. Place your face in my crootch, Higher ….. and I shall anoint thee with Lykwydd Narnya! I want your bespecktackled head inside me, ramming the gateway to my woomb. Twill be as comforting as a Fancie Feast in the Not-So-Great Hall of Szczmawgwhorets. Dream of your sweetheart, Ho Fang, or of Goldie-Boy Foockhart, or of whoever or whatever it takes to get you off! Or pleasure me with your Antagonystcyk 7000! Use your angry foock energie to resist the Unexceptional Curses ….. I often start casting spells spontaneously right before Whoregasm ….. so come prepared for a metamorphosis!

With the wicked whispers of a werewoolfian coocke whoore – Madame Saline

That evening, Madame Saline cast a long-distance Hermafrodeezyackal spell on Higher, giving him night dreams and nightmares that reverberated with the echo of her sadistick voice. The next day, Higher received a second letter from Madame Saline.....

Dear Higher,

As I mentioned in my previous letter, I'd like to take a ride on your Antagonystick 7000. Your face, my poosey, Higher. Deal? Physio-animate to Lost Angelist. Meet me at Fag-Greed's bungalow on Sunset ..... at sunset. Come to the cave Higher. There is meat and fire and it is warm! I might even invite a Sin-Torrid to join us. As I often say to Fag-Greed ..... "The More – The Fairie-Ur!" Physio-animate to Lost Angelist immediately! Everyone here is a lost soul posing as a wicked professional! So I can't help but crave your innocence! How I doth hunger for thy teenage man root! Come on up to Griffith Park! You'll be James Dean; I'll be Natalie Wood. You'll be Sal Mineo; I'll be Shelley Winters (Shelley Winters being more likely and frankly more doable in my case than Natalie Wood). I'll throw a lit match on some dry tinder and start a voracious wildfire. It's a perfeckt night for arson ….. the humiditie is unusually low ….. with the exception of that stormy ocean between my legs! I can hear the Santa Anaïs winds howling in the canyons. We'll treat ourselves to a boomp of coockaigne before we let the flames consume us in our final embrace of cremation – our Liebestod – to prepare us for our journey to Valhaha. If any Die-Fag-Anons happen to be creeping around in the brambles, I will instantly banish them to Morewhore with an Excludiatus Curse! And then they will die violently at the hands of vicious Blorks! HA HA HA HA HA HA HA!

I'm afraid that I have some sad news, Higher. Tomorrow, I must accompany Fag-Greed to the execution of Foockbeeck the Lipo-Creep at twilight. [J'adore le crépuscule!] I don't mean to frighten you Higher ….. but for me the death of the Lipo-Creep symbolizes Fag-Greed's imminent castration. And once he's out of the way ….. will the love of a voluptuous giantesse be too much for you Higher? Verily ….. I hopeth not! ….. Spending too much time down on your knees before Lord Quasibjzhorg again, Higher? Careful – lest unbeknownst you fall *under the influence of your stronger feminine side! I may just teach you a final lesson regarding submission. Don't underestimate me, Higher ….. I could easily metamorphose into a sorceresse-sized female praying mantis and bite off your head!*

Smotheringly, Suffocatingly – Madame Saline

The next evening, Madame Saline wrote a third letter – she was prolifick – this time to Whoremoania. Because men always betrayed Madame Saline ….. and only the love of a woman could make her feel truly complete …..

Dear Whoremoania,

I know that your mind is filled with phantasms of Goldie-Boy Foockhart, Vicktym Kloonck the Quispiszcz Professional and Frivolous Snide. But I see you as my captive mermaid, floating in an aquarium filled with margarine beer, in the green-black darkness of an Elvyszcz forest, lit only by occasional fireflies ….. Put away your childish Szczmoogle-Bjzhorg sex toys, Whoremoania ….. Hot poosey right this way! I can give you real love! Come to Mama!

SZCZMAWGWHORE(TS): A PORNOGRAPHICK BITCH-STORY

Fais-moi du plaisir! I won't be here in Snoregazmya, Nevada much longer, Whoremoania ….. I'm bound to fall into the Bottomless Pit of Middl Earf Hampton! The Dollblog is jealous of my decadent nature and so he wants to destroy me ….. Physio-animate here quickly! It's only a matter of time before I descend into the open jaws of the voracious maw of the Dollblog! I will fall from the tightrope like Nietzsche's Zarathustrian Payaso Oscuro! No worries, Whoremoania ….. Gondolphus Clownhouse, Morewhore's Ambassador from Middl Earf Hampton, will save me from the Dollblog. And I will live to be your Mrs. Robinson ….. I foocked Gondolphus years ago. I De-Fleured him! I sat on his face ….. I almost ass-fixiated him! My poosey is a volcanick thermal pool! Twas a short, brutish, bestial affair with Gondolphus ….. about 15 minutes long ….. I was never the marrying kind! Yes – I burned Clownhouse! But he'll come back for more like a fool who never learns from his mistakes. He will appear to repay this favor in my time of need …..

    I LÜV YOU AND I LOUVRE YOU !!!!

    Maleficently, Madame Saline

Three days later, after having read Madame Saline's letter and having thought it over, Whoremoania committed the ultimate ackt of rebellion by means of sorcerie acquired from Frivolous Snide. She physio-animated herself into the woomb of Madame Saline and commenced her study of *Szczmawgwhorets: A Pornographick Bitch-Story*. "Me want men not, me want men not, me want men not ….." Whoremoania chanted to herself in her palpitating prison. "Me want eternal witch-moomie koont-fort."

Three days later in the evening, Higher Parterre wrote about Madame Saline in his diarie …..

….. When Madame Saline finally had her way with me, everything became clear. I had been rescued from my virginal brouillard. She approached me with the glowing golden eyes of a hoorny poolyamoorous foock machine ….. all of a sudden we were soaring in the western skies of Amurycka Profunda. We flew from her executive penthouse at the Hellton like Ebenezer Scrooge and The Ghost of Christmas Past. We sailed over Snoregazmya, Nevada at sunset ….. thrilling to the wicked laughter

of its flambuoyant dancers, compulsive gamblers and transsexual prostitutes ..... then Madame Saline whisked me away from all of that horrifickally crass entertainment (she wanted to proteckt me as well ..... she respeckted my naïveté) ..... we laughed as we eavesdropped on the Evilangelists with our eagle-sharp eyes ..... as they secretly auto-eroticized with pornographie late at night ..... before waking up the next morning to their delusions of respecktabilitie and responsabilitie. Our X-ray vision afforded us superb viewing into the lairs of coyotes, wildcats and rattlers; rusty containers of bio-hazardous waste; diminishing ground water supplied by underground aquifers. Then we hovered over Poom Poom Spryngs with its deeply tanned, tattoo-covered, multi-pierced Toomb-of-Fäglandya clones as they indulged in toxick gossip springing from spiritually vackuous lives based solely on their carnal identities. We circumvented their circuit parties. We knew that the weapons of mass strucktion were down there somewhere ..... Madame Saline drooled in anticipation of gripping onto one of those boombs .....

whose circumference equaled that of a Yosemite redwood …..

EL SILENCIO DE MADAME SALINE

After her adventures with Higher and Whoremoania, Madame Saline was taken captive by Morewhorian Blorks and delivered to the Mergers and Acquisitions Secktion of the Legal Division of the Department of Cease and Desist in the Not-So-Great Hall of Che-Mary-Kay Foul-Thyng. Whereupon the Dollblog was summoned from its Abyss. Whereby Madame Saline was promptly stripped by the Blorks and then caned by the Dollblog Itself until she had lost consciousness. As a result of this torture ….. Madame Saline deteriorated, dissipated and then disintegrated into the mists of Galeeszczya. Wherein the Soul-Spirit-Geist energy of Madame Saline merged with that of Quasibjzhorg (AKA *He Who Would Not Be Loved*) within whose physickal entitie she remained trapped in a sublimated and vaporous form.

GLOWING GREEN GAS

Glowing Green Gas

On top of French Vanilla Mountain was Sweet Pumpkin Castle, the seat of power for the wealthy kingdom of Buzzantium – that was illuminated at night by a halo of Glowing Green Gas. The royalty of Buzzantium were partial to hot brown poo pie, the consumption of which caused them disturb the surrounding mountain air with their farts, creating a noxious atmosphere that satisfied their perverse sense of smell. This gaseous infiltration attracted swarms of Reptilian Raptors, known by the locals as Decrapitors – that frequently circled the castle hungering for human flesh. The inhabitants of the castle court, the Buzzantiites, possessed no extraordinary magical powers, save that of creative visualization – a trait that occurred naturally in their race. But the practice of creative visualization by the Buzzantiites had done nothing to abate the onslaught of Decrapitors. Thus the Buzzantiites had no choice but to resort to their ancient practice of sacrificing a virgin to Snore-On [the Dark Prince of Morewhore]. The day came when the court gathered around the latest victim – a young maiden by the name of Mailandia – to witness her physio-animation to Morewhore, where she would then be sucked into Snore-On's Giant Pink Eye. However, as it happened that Snore-On could not stand the taste of her purity, he spit her out so forcefully that she flew into the Bottomless Pit of Middl Earf Hampton – where the strength and function of her reptilian brain was tripled in capacity by her encounter with the Dollblog. She was then sold to the Blorks of Morewhore to be used as a concubine. And even though the Blorks were known to be so unsightly that any foreigner that looked upon them would turn to stone – Mailandia ended up enjoying sex with the Blorks, because the Dollblog had also destroyed her conscience.

The greedy Blorks used primitive coal-fed industrial mechanisms to power their nefarious factories that satisfied their ever-growing need for instant gratification. The noxious fumes created by Morewhore's industries were blown all the way to Buzzantium by Barbyzonya Solar-Wind, Goddess of Hyperventilation and Empress of Neglected Southern Gothic Traumas. Even though French Vanilla Mountain was thousands of miles away from Morewhore, the global warming that was a by-product of the Morewhorian pollution was heating up the atmosphere of the countryside surrounding Buzzantium.

In the quaint courtyard of Sweet Pumpkin Castle, the Buzzantiite lords and ladies shed frequent tears over the prospect of French Vanilla Mountain's eventual melting ….. "We dare not speak of the day when we will drown in the torrents of its creamy, sugary summit. Our Green Tea Ice Cream Planet was created in the Big Bang and we still feel the reverberations of that event by means of cosmic background radiation. We respect the mysterious forces that created this world of abundance – but we resent the possible inundation of phlegm-creating dairy that will destroy our people" ….. Though the Buzzantiites were not a hostile tribe – they were pragmatic. For that reason, they had erected a series of barbed wire fences around the base of the mountain so that none of the Lower Dwellers who salivated for the treasures of Buzzantium could venture in and contaminate the court with their work-worn hands.

The Lower Dwellers longed for the development of their neglected valley, which had come to be known as The Valley of Disillusionment. Unlike the Buzzantiites, they dreamt of the day when the sweet creamy summit of French Vanilla Mountain would flow down upon them in a delicious torrent. They imagined bathing themselves luxuriously in a gigantic beige lake, created by a dam that would have already been constructed if they had only had the resources. The Lower Dwellers held late-night meetings deep within their torch-lit caves where they vented their frustration ….. *Those aristocratic bitches in their ivory tower castle can protect themselves from the horror of our pain ….. with anti-depressants that we can't afford since we have no health insurance …..* Their loud nighttime heckling stemming from justified resentment frequently awoke the Buzzantiites from their deepest slumbers; they often shook with fear until sunrise …..

However, the lords and ladies of Sweet Pumpkin Castle had found a way to appease the angry inhabitants of the valley. A clever Buzzantiite had invented a machine that solidified Glowing Green Gas into the sugar and flour necessary to make Glowing Green Gas Pie. The aroma of the pies eventually enchanted all of the Lower Dwellers – sending them into opium-like trances that rendered them non-productive, non-complaining and non-threatening for weeks at a time. Glowing Green Gas Pie was the Achilles' heel of the Lower Dwellers – they became addicted to it; they were enslaved by its seductive powers. They knew it was bad for them; they knew it was the creation of their enemy. But they still could not resist it. Many of the Lower Dwellers participated in a Twelve Step program formed to help them overcome this addiction (although most of them denied that they ever had slips). Glowing Green Gas Pie was like a lover that was always available and ready to satisfy.

The Decrapitors relished these pies as much as the Lower Dwellers. The sweet intoxicating vapor of Glowing Green Gas Pie actually caused the

Decrapitors to produce fire in their respiratory systems. Consequently, they rained down jets of purple flame onto the main courtyard of Sweet Pumpkin Castle – so great was their desire for those pies – as well as for the poor unfortunates who happened to be caught out in the open, transporting boxes of Glowing Green Gas Pie from one section of the castle to another. But casualties were rare as pungent fire-repellent Shit Flower Trees had been planted in the castle courtyard. The iridescent brown, tan, and gold leaves of the Shit Flower Trees were also known for their ability to deflect the radiation – that emanated from the Green Tea Ice Cream Sun – back towards Morewhore [Morewhore had always been the hottest land on the Green Tea Ice Cream Planet]. The ever-increasing heat caused by the "Green Teahouse Effect" had made the Morewhorians so insanely angry that civil wars had broken out among their various factions.

The Decrapitors routinely hammered the Buzzantium castle walls with their fiercesome spiked tails. But the damage was negligible, as the castle walls were 30 feet deep with glass windows 15 feet thick. All of that had been constructed by the Buzzantiites after having learned the hard way that they had to invest in the protection of their real estate. The leader of the Decrapitors, Gregarious Egregious, made exuberant proclamations of reverence for Glowing Green Gas Pie – that had the opposite effect on the Decrapitors that it did on the Lower Dwellers. As well as causing them to produce fire – Glowing Green Gas Pie also made them excrete gold – that regularly rained down onto the Valley of Disillusionment. Over time, the Decrapitors had learned that they could lure the Lower Dwellers out into the open using their gold excrement as bait. However, those among the Lower Dwellers who were both the fastest and the most daring would sprint for the gold and then squirrel it away in their caves – creating capital for an eventual uprising against Buzzantium.

LULA BELL HASSENPFEFFER

Lula Bell Hassenpfeffer, the taciturn female leader of the Lower Dwellers, was not afraid of Gregarious Egregious. And she resented the local populations, specifically those among her own people who lusted after golden shit bricks ….. thus she pondered ….. *I don't need involvement in the worlds of neither men nor monster. I can be goin after what I wants in an Amazonian-like manner – takin no prisoners and wastin no time in doin it. Don't have no need of nothin bein stuck in my orifices. I am entirely self-sufficient. I am complete. If anyone were to surmise that I were jes a pliant, malleable feminine physical entity with a brain filled with inconsequential thoughts – then them would be sure to feel the brunt of my wrath. Gals that like team sports and contact sports ain't dumb. In fact – them is smarter than most women – cuz them gets to know better the strategic and warlike ways of men. And I don't need no Glowin Green Gas Pie. Glowin Green Gas Pie has its origins in sloth. I am jes fine with the orange, red and purple root vegetables that flourish in the rocky soil of the Valley of Disillusionment …..*

Though Lula Bell Hassenpfeffer's stern manner gave many of the Lower Dwellers the impression that she was heartless – in reality, she was also a giver. She could often be found stirring and watching over boiling porridge in a scalding cauldron near the mouth of her cave. She was known all around the region for this invigorating gruel and the Lower Dwellers risked death by Decrapitor to savor a taste of this as well. Lula Bell also prepared stacks of steaming pancakes for the clamoring hordes of Amazonians whose ranks had swelled among the Lower Dwellers. Hers were known to be the fluffiest pancakes in the land, as they were prepared with carbonated spring water that occurred naturally in the Valley of Disillusionment. The Amazonians, who were veterans from the wars along the border of Morewhore, had recently returned home after constructing an anti-immigration fence to discourage invasions by Blorks. Deep within their caves, they forged weapons of steel and crafted jewelry with precious stones. They created helmets, breastplates, shields and swords to protect them from all of their oppressors.

Lula Bell and the Amazonians lived apart from the world of men. And so ultimately the Lower Dwellers' society had become a matriarchal one. The men folk took care of the children and made clothes. They washed pots and pans in nearby icy mountain streams, though only under the moonlight, as the

Decrapitors never attacked at night. After the Amazonians' ranks grew to that of a majority among the Lower Dwellers, many of them became intoxicated by their newfound positions of power within the societal hierarchy. As the men folk performed their domestic chores, they were taunted by the Amazonians in their belligerent language of Ipodia.....

"SLAVE, THY LONELINESS, THY MUNDANE SADNESS AMUSETH US! TIS THE BEAUTY OF OUR ISOLATED CULTURE! NEVER THINK THAT THY WORK HATH ENDED, SLAVE! AN ETERNAL ABUNDANCE OF IT AWAITETH THEE! IF THOU EVER THINKEST OF REBELLING AND ESCAPING, THOU SHALT BE QUICKLY CAPTURED AND WE SHALL CHAIN THY QUIVERING BODIES TO THE ROCKS TO BE EXPOSED AND THEN DEVOURED BY DECRAPITORS! ..... ONE OF OUR ELDER SISTERS DIED YESTER EVENTIDE. SHE WILL BURN ON A PYRE BEFORE SHE SENT IS OVER THE WATERFALL DESTINED FOR VALHAHA! ..... SUCH A FATE AWAITETH US ALL WHETHER WE BE AMAZONIAN OR SUBMISSIVE MALE. DEATH KNOWETH NO SEXISM! DEATH IS LIKE THE BLACK CAT THAT SAUNTERS DOWN THE SHADOWY PATHS OF THE NARNYAN LANTERN WAYSTE. THE BLACK CAT DEATH IS THE QUEEN OF ARCHAIC NIGHT.

BARBYZONYA SOLAR-WIND, GODDESS OF HYPERVEN-TILATION AND EMPRESS OF NEGLECTED SOUTHERN GOTHIC TRAUMAS, IS OUR EMPATH. SHE ABSORBETH OUR EMOTIONAL OVERFLOW IN YE TEMPLE OF THE DEITIE OF YE OLDE ENGLYSHE LEATHER ….."

Lula Bell Hassenpfeffer ended her exhausting days secure in the recesses of her comfortable cave. To protect her from being poisoned by the increasingly vindictive male population of the Lower Dwellers, eunuchs tasted her food and wine and tended the fires whose crackling soothed her like a lullaby. Every night, she prayed to the Hawk Headed Goddess and then drifted off to sleep. Lula Bell knew deep down that loving actions towards all of the inhabitants of her land contributed to her bank account of good karma, as well as to the greater good of the collective unconscious. Nonetheless ….. to live everyday life in the Valley of Disillusionment ….. solely by such a karmic code and without pragmatism ….. would have been downright naïve.

GONDOLPHUS
CLOWNHOUSE

Gondolphus Clownhouse

Gondolphus Clownhouse was a ghostwriter who went by the pen name of Thumbert Smotherford. Thumbert Smotherford, the metaphor, represented Gondolphus' sexual shame. Thumbert was a lonely, obese, bespectacled professor lacking sexual confidence and the nerves of steel that characterized true men of the streets – who banged their bitches, boys or bitch boys with uninhibited bravado after a hard day's work building luxurious upper-class urban skyscrapers. They were real men who weren't tormented by their inner lives, because they were too busy helping others to ever consider taking antidepressants. In their downtime, these macho specimens also enjoyed fetishizing every aspect of their sexuality. And they did so without giving a second thought to any subsequent guilt.

Gondolphus Clownhouse had been born into wealth in the last days of Amurycka Profunda's aristocracy. A symptom of that background was Gondolphus' innately condescending attitude towards the working class, with whom he had had little contact prior to his departure at age 20 from the village of his upbringing. He had been the classic geek: straight A student, member of the Honor Society, teacher's pet, always ready with a raised hand when no-one else in class knew the answer. He was introverted, virginal, apathetic about sports – a physical coward. He was still sucking his thumb at his graduation ceremony. He had been traumatized in high school when his male classmates laughed at his microscopic penis in the showers after gym class. Gondolphus became a writer to get revenge on them. So far, that was proving to be a very difficult life. Unfortunately, he had lacked the aggressive nature that is required for managing hedge funds.

After years of writing as Thumbert Smotherford, Gondolphus Clownhouse came to co-exist with

Thumbert within the shared confines of their psychic mental plane. When Gondolphus looked into the mirror, he saw Thumbert, who looked like a cross between Divine and Alfred Hitchcock. Gondolphus was severely judgmental of Thumbert, who he characterized as "one of those goddam bleeding heart liberals, who feels sorry for kids who grew up in the projects, but who wouldn't be caught dead in their neighborhood".

Gondolphus lived a life of Ralph Nader-esque frugality upstairs from the Kryspy Kreem on Snore-On Boulevard in downtown Szczmawgford-on-Avon-Laidie. Gondolphus was the current night manager of this Kryspy Kreem. The store was patronized by super-sized women whose tight-fitting pastel polyester pants cruelly revealed their grossly bloated abdomens, gigantic asses and the corrugated topography of their panty lines. They came to Kryspy Kreem to console themselves after hemorrhaging money at the local casino ..... The delicious smells of Kryspy Kreem helped to distract Gondolphus from the hours that he spent correcting the papers of his mediocre students, whose education was being financed by part-time careers as straight-acting hoostlers [Gondolphus was a professor of general studies at Szczmawgweed Academy for Boys, where homosexuality was practiced but never discussed]. *How I envy their lack of conscience ….. he sighed ….. It is my fervent hope that one of these weekends ….. one of these teen hoostlers will step into my Chartreuse Hybrid Priapus and accept my cash payment for their services ….. Sometimes at night,* Gondolphus liked to park his car on Krissuhfuh Street, the main venue of the queer part of town. It was there that he waited for his *banjee boys* ….. so full of adrenalin that he wasn't concerned about the risk. He needed this euphoria to banish his fear, as he was simply not brash enough to forthrightly express his point-of-view in a face-to-face conversation with another man. Especially when he was attracted to that *male object …..*

When feeling creatively blocked, Gondolphus would pray to the Ghost of Christine Jorgensen ….. OH CHRISTINE! PLEASE HELP ME TO ACHIEVE MY CREATIVE, ARTISTIC AND PROFESSIONAL GOALS ….. was one of his typical prayers. Although he was a spiritual man, he chose not to participate in any organized religion.

Pray as Gondolphus frequently did to his transsexual deity, he was unable to transcend his jealousy of hot, body-fascist queers. This issue consumed him, but he was too lazy to do the necessary workouts that would give him the Chelsea Hottie Girlymann body of his dreams. And even with his spanking-new ripped physique, he would still have to do battle with his gnawing doubts and incessant insecurities ..... not to mention his interminable conflict with Thumbert. *I want to be loved as I am!* ..... Gondolphus wailed to the heavens before stuffing another kruller into his face. One of his favorite ways of dealing with stress was to curl up on his couch with a box of double chocolate doughnuts and whisper to himself ..... *Foock it! I'll settle for the gluttonous excess of Jobba the Koont* ..... And when that became too oppressive, he would stroll along the lonely, lamp lit pathways of the local park ..... where gay-for-pay ruled the night .....

Gondolphus never marched in gay pride parades. He told himself that he didn't need a rainbow flag to define his existence. He had convinced himself that his fear of crowds had made him claustrophobic. The toxic combination of in-your-face sexuality and artifice displayed during those parades sent Gondolphus into a downward spiral of shame, desire and torment. He felt too vulnerable to obtain either what he wanted or needed. He detested the object of his desire for making him feel so sexual. He had always been a submissive bottom in his fantasy life. And he had always been unhappy that he had been born a man. He had considered getting a sex change as a teenager – as he had viewed his attraction to men as being just plain wrong. And since he couldn't face the humiliation of being the pussy-boy of his dream top – fantasy and masturbation had to suffice. Because he could not accept and make peace with his feminine side – he ended up being ruled by it instead.

Then – after a terrifying encounter with the Dollblog in the Bottomless Pit of Middl Earf Hampton – everything changed. Gondolphus' brush with death had given him a new outlook on life. He let go of his petty obsessions with the Self and became a concerned citizen of ecologically-challenged Szczmawgford-on-Avon-Laidie. Gondolphus was now willing to step outside of himself long enough to take actions that would contribute to the rehabilitation of the Blue

Green Planet ….. and so he ruminated ….. *Dammit! When are they going to find another world with a breathable atmosphere and drinkable water in this solar system? How I wish that the Blue Green Planet had a colon so that it could be flushed out with an enema! Why can't we just shoot all of this hazardous waste out into the absolute zero of deep space ….. I long for the serenity of Antarktikskaya. It is a useless continent ….. It is my hope that all of the garbage of the Blue Green Planet will be transported to Antarktikskaya to be irradiated and purified by the gigantic hole in the ozone layer above it …..*

After gradually having put into practice behaviors consistent with the higher version of himself, Gondolphus finally put down the first sentences of his latest novel in writing, which were as follows: "Oh Paris and Berlin! How I doth love thee with your gay mayors, your refined sense of smell, your contemplative cafés and your Love Parade. I love your department stores, your Metro, your bookishness, your minimal interest in television, the pensive voiceovers of your documentaries, your multilingual hoostlers and your functional Green Party! No matter how hard I try to perfect my

French ..... I am unworthy. Quell me like Quasimodo. Eradicate me like Esmeralda ..... *je fais tant de fautes, ça va mal ..... je suis un ange ..... passé* ..... Your Parisians laugh at my Amurycka Profundan accent! But I will read *Le Monde* and listen to *Radio France Internationale* ..... until I speak with the authority of Charles de Gaulle ..... until I have mastered the fluid vernacular of Edith Piaf. Then I'll strap myself onto an atomic bomb and I'll fly out into deep space and dematerialize into pure energy! Then I will die happy! As for German ..... *ich kann das auch nicht so gut machen* ..... although no-one cares about my lack of German fluency in the darkrooms of those rubber fetish sex-clubs in Berlin. So I'm going to stop putting pressure on myself and start trying to enjoy life. Just because I'm an ignorant Amurycka Profundan doesn't mean that I can't spice up my life with a little danger! Europeans are so much more forgiving when it comes to vices! And there's no shortage of chubby chasers on any continent who will pursue me for my zaftig, voluptuous figure ..... *La vie est comme ça! Es tut mir leid!* Talk to me like a left-leaning Libertarian and I'll listen to you ..... Otherwise ..... *allez-y! Heraus!*"

The stress of 21st century living – combined with his complexes, fears and worries – prompted Gondolphus to pray to another powerful Goddess ..... Maya Hiyuh Powuh ..... *OH MAYA HIYUH POWUH! GRANT ME GUIDANCE IF THAT BE THY WILL. I AM AN EMPTY VESSEL THAT WAITETH TO BE FILLED. MY CONSTRUCTIVE SOLITUDE HATH EVOLVED INTO VEGETATIVE ISOLATION. WHERE IS MY CARNAL REWARD, MISTRESS MAYA? IF I DON'T GET MY REWARD SOON, I'M GOING TO GO ON A SEX BINGE! AND IT WON'T BE WORTH IT UNLESS I PICK UP ONE OF THOSE ANTIBIOTIC RESISTANT STAPH INFECTIONS!*

Maya Hiyuh Powuh heard every word of Gondolphus' prayers. She responded with the following advice in the gruff voice of a heavy smoker ..... *Stuff your balls inside a ruby slipper ..... then tie it up tightly with leather shoelaces. Indulge yourself in the pain ..... clothe yourself in a hair shirt ..... dismiss your lustful leanings as being animalistic ..... revert to the ways of medieval Christendom ..... only then will your chastitie be fully realized .....*

..... *THANK YOU, MAYA HIYUH POWUH! I AM PRESENT, I AM IN THE MOMENT, I AM HERE NOW. AND I*

AM BREATHING! I BREATHE IN THROUGH MY MOUTH! I BREATHE OUT THROUGH MY ASSHOLE! IN ABSORBING YOUR GUIDANCE, I DISPEL THE DEMONS THAT RENDER ME UNWORTHY OF YOUR NIRVANA. CREATIVITY IS ITS OWN REWARD! ALL OF THE CHAKRA COLORS ARE MIXING IN MY CHAMBER OF COMBINATION NATIVE AMURYCKA PROFUNDAN AND QUEBECOIS CLOWN MASK. AND IF ALL OF THOSE COLORS COMBINE TO BECOME BLACK – THAT WILL WORK FOR ME! BLACK IS ALWAYS CLASSIC – THEY LOVE IT IN ROME! EVEN THOUGH I AM NOT A MATERIALIST – I SAW A BLACK AND DARK GRAY HUGO BOSS SUIT IN THE WINDOW OF A SHOP NEAR THE VIA CORSO – AND I JUST HAD TO HAVE IT! IT WAS PERFECT FOR MY LATEST GAY-FOR-PAY TRICK! [YOU DON'T THINK THAT I WOULD BUY IT FOR MYSELF – DO YOU?] I ACQUIESCED TO THE OBSESSION! I AM UNDAUNTED! I AM LETTING GO OF ALL OF MY DEFENSES! I TAKE WHAT WORKS FOR ME AND LEAVE THE REST!

Gondolphus took a moment to daydream while surveying the passersby on Snore-On Boulevard from the comfort of his second-story window. Twas Christmas time and even though snow was falling softly and gently onto the streets of the village ..... all was not well in this faux-idyllic world. Delightful homespun carolers were having their faces smashed in by an invasion of brutal Morewhorian Blorks. This had been going on for years – so much so that the residents of Szczmawgford-on-Avon-Laidie had become desensitized to the violence, preferring to exist in a state of low-grade fear, rather than one of compassionate activism. As long as its citizens had money in their coffers – none of them complained.....

MEANWHILE IN
THE TEMPERATE LAND OF SHRILL

In the temperate land of Shrill, not far from the quaint Siberianism of Szczmawgford-on-Avon-Laidie, gay and bisexual porn stars were now taking golf holidays. Once shunned by the purveyors of the Morally Superior Code, these former hedonists had finally gained admittance to the inner circle of the Puritan Pantheon. They had earned their capital and they intended to spend it. These hot, humpy men – along with the occasional vampy vixen and the odd gossip columnist fag hag – swung their clubs with erotic vigor in every sexy megalopolis on the Blue Green Planet. But this kind of lifestyle change did not come without sacrifice. These former porn stars were now starving on a sexless Twelve Step diet. They were horny satyrs masquerading as benevolent saints. They were living a lie. They had no interest in the notion of truth. They just wanted to get back to their tradition of fantasy, secrets, and manipulation. As much as they tried to be spiritual – they couldn't survive without the high of transgression. In reaction to this trend, Evilangelism and anti-intellectualism were flourishing in Shrill. A zone of political pragmatism sprang up in which book burnings were now well attended by decadent pagans as well as Evilangelists – factions otherwise intolerant of one another. Violent video games had replaced the dusty old Western canon. Which was fine with the Evilangelists. Their goal was complete denial of the reptilian brain – that would eventually result in violence born from the frustration of thwarted and repressed sexual expression. The Evilangelists were creating a blueprint for the secession of Jah-Hee-Zeus-Land. They dreamt of creating a sterile, spic and span confederacy. This plan was described in an excerpt from their latest manifesto ….. *Comrades! It will no longer be necessary to take hot smelly dumps in disgusting Trans-Siberian railroad bathrooms. The Evilangelists have acquired ownership of the Polar-Express. Burl Ives is our king! Rudolph the Red-Nosed Reindeer is our John the Baptist! Herbie the Dentist is our Saint Francis! And the spirit of Fandy Whorehole is our Saint Augustine.*

BACK IN SZCZMAWGFORD-ON-AVON-LAIDIE

The following evening, after having dropped his pen in exhaustion, Gondolphus dreamt of acid rivers running down from the volcanic mountains of Morewhore to the rolling green hills outside of Szczmawgford-on-Avon-Laidie ….. *Woe to the unfortunate who attempted to wade across those acid rivers barefoot. They were left with stubs for feet ….. if they were lucky. Most toppled over and dissolved, hissing and boiling, howling in agony ….. without ever reaching the opposite bank. The last thing they saw before leaving the Blue Green Planet was a violent orange sunset* behind distant purple peeks ..... as if Mother Nature was peering out from behind those mountains, giggling cruelly. In the moment of her choosing ..... all it took was a wave of Mother Nature's hand to significantly decrease the surplus population of a Blue Green Planet that was full to bursting. The voices of Maya Hiyuh Powuh, the Hawk-Headed Goddess and Barbyzonya Solar-Wind, Goddess of Hyperventilation and Empress of Neglected Southern Gothic Traumas, could be heard in the background ..... screaming in unison at ear-piercing volume ..... their dissonant shrieking intermingling with that of early 70s folk-rock harmonies inspired by Crosby, Stills and Nash ..... TOO MUCH PEOPLE! FUCKIE SUCKIE MAKE YOU DIE! IN DREAM YOU LIVE LONG TIME! BLUE GREEN PLANET BYE BYE!

DJZHEEMI SPARKS

Djzheemi Sparks

Banished to a living room with mustard-colored carpet to listen to 70s rock under the headphones – this is where Djzheemi Sparks dreamt of revenge. His rage had become so intolerable that it had transformed itself into a fantastic prison submerged in an emotionally frozen lake. Djzheemi was tortured by his dreams. In his latest ..... *a subzero draft was blowing under the door into a garage that was connected to an upper-middle class, wood-paneled, sepia-colored, linoleum-tiled suburban kitchen. In this garage ..... gray white brown soot and ice bled from the pine green 1977 Chevy Nova tire tracks onto the cement. From here, Djzheemi was led through a wormhole by an mysterious force ..... he became transfixed by an incandescent blue-violet cold fire that pulled him towards an unknown destination. Suddenly, he was box-cutting a hole in the ground of a high contrast landscape punctuated by ultra-white birch trees. A hand reached up and dragged him down ..... he had been snatched away by the Zalphagamorian, a bronze-colored creature with a scaly marbleized hide. The Zalphagamorian then ushered Djzheemi into a subterranean chamber that lead towards the dressing room of Fräulein Baikalskaya's nightclub "K-Hole Sloot Rehab" [this place being an important symbol in a premonition of Djzheemi's future life] ..... where Djzheemi would be prepared for his sexual lobotomy .....*

..... The Zalphagamorian stripped off Djzheemi's clothes quickly and efficiently and stuffed his bare ass into a chilled pot o' gold at the end of a black and white rainbow ..... that Zalphagamorian's Pumpkin Trolls then gleefully pulled out from under him ..... leaving him bewildered ..... as their laughter echoed throughout the underground cave. Then Djzheemi, the Pumpkin Trolls and the Zalphagamorian sailed down a deep, meandering aqua rabbit-hole, buffeted by warm breezes from below, to land at the feet

of Zauberfeuer ..... who was holding court in the main hall of a castle that sparkled with gold, silver, torches and disco balls ..... it was a room whose floors, ceilings and walls were comprised of mirrors ..... Zauberfeuer, a pleasure-seeking hedonist who resembled a more decadent version of The Ghost of Christmas Present, introduced himself to Djzheemi and then proceeded to question him in a deep yet faggy-sexy voice ..... I am Zauberfeuer. Are you searching for the Hole of Blood, my son? Or is it The Chocolate Cave you seek? Is it your wish to mop up the Afterbirth of the Blood-Shit Koont? ..... he demanded jovially ..... I don't care about your brain, Djzheemi. And you won't either after the soothing effects of your sexual lobotomy kick in .....

..... Djzheemi blushed, mortified with shame. He ran away to hide in a dark corner. The Pumpkin Trolls pursued him, jeering him, tickling him and shrieking with laughter. Zauberfeuer laughed right along with them. Tears ran down Djzheemi's cheeks as he sucked his thumb. After about a minute of this, Djzheemi started shaking with fear ..... then he covered his ears with his hands and screamed ..... why *was this happening ..... what was to become of him? Seeing him in this pathetic condition, Zauberfeuer and The Pumpkin Trolls laughed even more hysterically .....* "OH ISN'T HE ADORABLE! DROWNING IN HIS SELF-PITY! WHAT WILL YOU DO WHEN THE CAVE GETS DARKER, DJZHEEMI? WHAT WILL YOU DO WHEN WE GO BEYOND THE REACH OF UPPER-WORLD LIGHT?"

Zauberfeuer was Djzheemi's opposite. He had befriended his animal nature long ago and was therefore not overpowered by it. Djzheemi, on the other hand, used fear and pain as drugs to numb out what little joy he had in his life. Djzheemi started analyzing to block out the torment ..... *Though it goes against my will ..... I am forced to admit it ..... Zauberfeuer is on the right track. The scolding Judeo-Christian God betrayed me by using me as his vessel. Whereas by praying to Zoë, the Reptilian Pit Bull ..... for Christ's sake, I can live again! I feel a secret joy when I use the name of Lord Szczmawg in vain!* REVEAL YOURSELF TO ME NOW, ZOË ..... EMBRACE ME LIKE KALI-SHIVA CREATOR-DESTROYER ..... I AM READY TO ACQUIESCE! ..... He woke up sweating, shouting, hyperventilating and unaware of his surroundings. Djzheemi pulled himself together after a few minutes and then tried to feel grateful for the life that he hated. He finally fell asleep a couple of hours before dawn.

Djzheemi Sparks was oblivious to the brilliant sunshine that awakened him. The only thing that got him through the day was his obsessions. Djzheemi suffered from the delusion that he had been nominated for an Oscar for his portrayal of a character named Robert Violence – in an under-the-radar film called *Mabel's Perfect Mince Pie*. Djzheemi needed this Oscar fantasy to survive – as he was very unpopular at his day job selling violent video games at Geek-Surv on West 14th Street near Soviet Union Square, Nueva Jork. In his mind, he was a closeted monster drag queen clown who did his makeup in the dark. Because it made more sense to him to get it wrong. He was living a double life. On weekends, Djzheemi donned his frilly white *I've Written a Letter to Daddy* party dress, a blonde wig with pre-atomic curls, delicate white ankle socks and white patent leather shoes. Then he ran across Central Park via 66th Street in that outfit ..... screaming curses, obscenities and racial epithets at the top of his lungs. Every time that he did this .....

he made it out of the park without being murdered ..... the sheer insanity of his energy having acted as a forcefield to keep all of the lowlife of that dark foonky park away from him. Fear was the only thing that made him feel truly alive. The exhilaration, adrenalin and danger granted him access to his stunted erotic nature.

ROBERT VIOLENCE

Robert Violence, Djzheemi's alter ego, had grown up in Downey, California – where he had been strongly influenced by the banal and mundane elements of Amurycka Profundan culture. In the opening scene of *Mabel's Perfect Mince Pie* ..... Robert is lying in a bathtub filled with shit prune wine mud ..... dreaming of creating pop singles with the following titles that were too inaccessible for the charts ..... *Chocolate Ass Pie, My Dad Wears a Diaper* and *Where Pink Becomes Brown*. As Robert is consumed with rage and completely devoid of social finesse ..... the only way for him to make it will be ..... via murder. He hires the homeless to work at his fledging record company. Robert watches their eyes light up at the prospect of free meals. Then after having them blindfolded and tortured by his henchmen ..... they are stabbed in their stomachs, stuffed into burlap bags and rolled down the sides of steep canyons not far from Müllholland Drive, Lost Angelist. No one cares about these casualties ..... they are a subgroup of a demographic that has fallen through the cracks and that will not be missed. Typically, they are vagabonds of Southern California beaches who have chugged massive quantities of vodka, suffered from hideous sunburns and frequented degenerate hotels in downtown Lost Angelist .....

BACK TO DJZHEEMI'S WORLD

At the end of the day, Djzheemi found himself immersed in a flashback from his traumatic childhood ..... "Maw, whar's Paw? Him gonna join us fer fudge poo pie tonight? Whar him at? Him at that thar shit doctor?" Djzheemi's maw were known as Evil Matilda. Her responded in a concerned-like manner ..... "Now let's be growed up bout this, Djzheemi. Him ain't called no shit doctor. Him are a procterologist and him are givin Paw some internal anaesthetic so that him can be right comforbibble while that thar procterologist sticks a tube up his asshole lookin for them thar cancer bumps." "Ahm uh skeered, Maw. If Paw's passed out, him won't know what's goin on. What if that thar procterologist stuck somethin else up thar ..... like big ole nukyelur warhead?" "Don't you worry none, honey buns. Lord Szczmawg will protect our Paw. That thar procterologist him got to do his job or Lord Szczmawg will strike him down." "Maw, how's that tube gonna find them thar cancer bumps?" "That tube's gotta camera on the end that takes pictures all the way up and down the winding tunnel that ends up at yer asshole." .....

..... "Daddy's at that age now whar him'll be gettin this done on a regular-like basis. I jes hope that that thar Grim Reaper ain't waitin down by the corner with his bony claws gripped roun the wall keepin a lookout fer Paw ..... laughin to himself and sayin ..... *You gotta way from me this time ..... I ain't comin fer ya yet, but one don't never know ..... when I'll be comin back fer yuh ..... GRIM REAPER'S COMIN FER*

YUH, BABY! THERE'S NO GUARANTEE YOU'LL BE HERE TOMORROW! YOU AIN'T NOTHIN BUT COSMIC DUST, HONEY CHILD! ALL IT TAKES IS ONE SHININ MOMENT FER ME TO DISTILL ALL YOU EEZ DOWN INTO DUST IN THE PALM OF MY COLD, BONEY HAND ….. AND THEN POOF! YOU'LL BE ALL BLOWED AWAY!" …..

….. "Don't cry little babies ….. even though Paw him were upset by that thar colonosocopy. The procterologist done told Paw that him warn't through and through clean. Him humiliarated Paw ….. and Paw couldn't help like feelin like a dirty shit-filled bein ….. even though Paw cleans out his asshole ever lovin day ….. him gives himself a daily enema with colon cleansers and various healthful concoctions." …..

….. "One night, as Paw caressed me in the master bedroom under the pale blue light of a full moon ….. him looked tenderly into my eyes and whispered ….. "I've always known that one day I'd be the King of Shit Mountain. So I'm gonna take me a dump on this here bed and then I'm gonna shove yer face right in it!" As I cried jazzy golden tears ….. Paw blowed out a big pungent skunk fart. And I were mad as the Dollblog and I done transformed myself into an incarnation of that creature ….. I whipped Paw real good and burned him right proper with my tentacles of fire. It were as if Paw and I was fightin in the Bottomless Pit of Middl Earf Hampton ….. suddenly the room were blazin with yellow-orange incandescence. And as the curtains was open, the neighbors done saw and heard our cataclysmic spectacle. Usns re-emerged from our pyrotechnical conflict as black and white wizards that was cleansed of all pride and shame ….. usns had become paragons of virtue and integrity (well at least fer that night). The next day, as I was standin in line at Tops supermarket ….. I felt my original sin snakin back up inside me like the xylem and phloem of Yggdrasil ….. then I took a peek inside Pipple Magazine and the ugly reality of the Blue Green Planet come back to me full force and returned me to the present moment ….."

DUNCAN DOONKEL HEISS

It were chow time and Djzheemi's Granny hollered fer him to get his bones along to the supper table. Her hollerin done always embarrassed him ….. "Satan's red, white and blue balls Granny! Yer carnival barker wails would re-animate the dearly departed!" "C'mon now, Djzheemi! Granny won't abide no criticism tonight! We're havin shit poo pie, maple sugar mud pecan pie and chocolate dirt worm beetle tart." Djzheemi loved all kinds of brown confections and delicacies ….. be they hot, steamy, smelly, sweet or bitter. As a child, him and his little friends had converted the backyard sandbox into a giant tray of mud shit sewage brownies. Granny lived on a farm nearby. Signs that read no trespassin was posted roun the perimeter of her property. Yet her had tempted Djzheemi to enter that forbidden zone jes the same ….. "I got big piles of cowshit fer ya here, Djzheemi ….. fer yer favorite sweet smelly brown cookies." her would wail. To make matters worse, her perverted old handyman, Duncan Doonkel Heiss, stepped up to assist her ….. "DUNCAN DOONKEL HEISS DOES THE MENACIN ROUN HERE WHEN THE WIDE-EYED ACT BIGGER THAN THEY BRITCHES!" exhorted Granny ….. "Jes remember that in the eyes of Lord Szczmawg, all homosexuals is an abomination. Hope ya don't got no plans to be wit mens!" ….. Djzheemi were mighty confused by Granny's outburst, as Duncan Doonkel

Heiss clearly had his eye on him. When Doonkel Heiss gazed upon Djzheemi, he saw fresh meat in need of corruption. Whereas Djzheemi suppressed his natural urges towards mens fer fear of losin the approval of his belligerent Granny. At that moment him were so overwhelmed by his attraction to Duncan Doonkel Heiss ….. that him become feverish and sweaty with shame. Vomit exploded from his gut right onto the compost heap. When him were finished, him took a moment to catch his breath, then him delved into a fantasy of an aristocratic grandmother from the 1920's ….. posin by her grand piano draped in pearls and serenely naked in an elegant, spacious stone mansion. Because bein with his real-life granny were jes too much to take ….. "Lord Szczmawg on high done cursed me with this here grandma that growed up out the groun like a knobbly patater. And I don't want to heed her unwise words no more!"

FILBERT SPARKS

As fer Djzheemi's brother Filbert ….. him had brought such shame upon the family that him were never spoken of. That is, until one day when him had to be forcibly removed from the premises – due to the imminent danger caused by his psychotic rage. Filbert were taken to the maximum-security ward of the local psychiatric hospital. As the orderlies held down Filbert on the cold stainless steel table fer his straitjacket fittin, his bloodcurdlin screams reached the upper edge of the stratosphere. Filbert reminisced bout his Paw with the orderlies ….. "Ain't nothin wrong with Paw's colon! In fact, as I remember it ….. Paw's mistresses considered his colon to be an aphrodisiac. I pray to the Übermenschen Deities that the size of his prostate will remain constant throughout eternity ….. I always respected Paw cuz when I were little him brung me whatever toys that I wanted. Didn't matter whether them was macho or girly. And him had a game that him liked to play with me that went somethin like this ….. here's what him used to say to me ….. "DAMMIT! I'M GONNA SHUT YOU UP AND SPOIL YOU ROTTEN! IN THE MEANTIME, I'LL START UP THE PINE GREEN 1977 CHEVY NOVA. THEN YOU GO OUT INTO THE GARAGE, PUT YER GODDAM MOUTH ON THE EXHAUST PIPE AND BREATHE IN THEM THAR

TOXIC PROTESTANT WORK ETHIC CARBON MONOXIDE FARTS!" …..

….. The red-faced orderlies was growin impatient with Filbert and his incomprehensible tirades. And so them sent fer his maw, Evil Matilda. Filbert sure done feared her smotherin ….. "Now hear me, Filbert" (Evil Matilda's soothin voice never disguised her severity) – "Drink the goddamn institutionalized milk and eat the rock-hard chocolate cake or I'll stuff yer mouth full of fine organic ash volcanic mudslide pureed molé tiramisu." ….. Filbert's exaggerated perception of the horror that were Matilda soon exhausted him. His screams and shouts dissipated ….. his stutterin and sputterin diminished ….. his anxiety lessened. Raised on snuff films, him had recently started listenin to Christian rock. Him drifted off into a daydream from his days of sanity ….. *him were at his high school's Sadie Hawkins dance. The local bumpkins, hooligans and country squires was kickin up they heels. The joyous song of a mad fiddler played in the background* …..

….. Filbert couldn't remember the words of that vile tune, but the melody stayed with him like a new best friend. Later that night, after Filbert finally fell into an anti-psychotic sleep ..... Djzheemi were right relieved. Djzheemi went home and then settled into slumber as well ..... *Him dreamt that him were at Santa's workshop at the North Pole. Mrs. Santa were in the kitchen starin through the frosted windowpanes with her kaleidoscope. Her were watchin Djzheemi bouncin up and down on Santa's lap. But her dared not interrupt Santa in his workshop because her feared that red-faced wrath that erupted from within him whenever him were caught engaged in his secret pleasures. Djzheemi wouldn't have to ask fer any presents this year ..... because him were gettin his right now. And soon him would pay the naughty boy price. In a couple of days, Djzheemi would be burnin with rectal gonorrheal fire. Nonetheless, in the heat of the moment, Djzheemi whispered into Santa's ear ..... "I acted real bad this year so that you'd put coal in my stockin ..... and then treat me like shit!" Then Santa shot his golden load across the room (him believed in safer sex) multitaskin in the process by glazin them thar Christmas decorations that was ready to be baked in the kiln. Mrs. Santa were so inspired by Santa's performance that her smeared pumpkin pies onto her ass cheeks. Then her stripped off her clothes and jumped into a swimmin pool in the backyard that were full of mincemeat and cranberry orange relish. While savorin the sticky sweetness ….. her heard gunshots. A gang of killer Blorks from Morewhore had jes driven by in they low-rider and had gunned down Santa's elves that was hard at work at the time makin toys. Upon hearin and seein all of this ….. a green dragon of vengeance overtook Mrs Santa's spirit. Her metamorphosed into a nuclear mushroom cloud ….. vaporizin the Northern Hemisphere and settin off a chain of events that heated up the Blue Green Planet to 424° Fahrenheit. The oceans boiled off quickly ….. and the human race and all of the other sentient beins of the Blue Green Planet ….. who was not pulverized soon thereafter ….. died pantin, scorched, dehydrated and suffocatin …..*

THE TRAVAILS OF GINGER BOCEY

THE TRAVAILS OF GINGER BOCEY

Her name were Ginger Bocey, her wore a sequin maroon tube top, purple velvet pants and platform shoes with macramé straps and soles of cork. Her were glam-rockin out in her countrified way. There were a stain on them pants along the ass crack from where a pack of prepubescents had attacked her with a chocolate ice cream cone. That were before her had developed her special powers. Her wore them dirty pants with pride, her warn't no society lady, her life were dirty and her rubbed it in everone's face. It were known in the neighborhood that her had been defiled by Conniver Witherhyde in an old VW van. With her eyebrows, nose, lips, tongue and navel pierced – her resembled that blue-black-haired, blue-eyed, pale-faced sorceress from *The Kräft*. Her roamed the dark highways roun Smellicottville, a farm town in upstate New York. Inevitably, her picked up the wrong kind of trucker durin forays that led to trysts in rest areas or local country parks – where one time by choice her were violated on a picnic table. The incident were seen as a silhouette in a shaft of light emanatin from the door to the nearby disgustin cement lavatories. "Damn ….. splinters in my ass again!" her sighed as her brute of the moment hightailed it off into the pitch-black night. Her rested her black and blue ass on the parkin lot gravel that were made hot by the friction of big black trucker tires …..

….. Ginger made her way back to Smellicottville, where badass bikers was havin a coke binge on the second floor of the Genesee Saloon. Music were playin inside ….. "When I hear them Appalatchin harmonies – I wanna make a porno!" Ginger crowed like a brain-damaged Evilangelist as her opened the door to the joint. As soon as her entered the place, her mood ring turned black – a sure sign that powers of the occult was operatin in the vicinity. Them bikers looked up at her stupified and her played dumb as her gave them introduction ..... "HI MY NAME'S GINGER AND I'M A PISCES." Her then stuck out her tongue, stripped down to her birthday suit and did a back bend on the pool table in homage to Soviet gymnasts that her had worshipped as a child – when her had still been dreamin about bein somebody. Afore the pressure put on her by her ignorant, abusive family bore down on her like a car-crushin junkyard machine and turned her into a no-good. The strobe light came on and *Highway to Hell* started playin on the jukebox. That were the last thing Ginger remembered that night – which is how her preferred it ..... *Ah jes shut down and let the dark demons take over .....* her were known to say. Durin that lost weekend, Jah-Hee-Zeus come to her in a dream durin a fitful post-coital nap ..... *her were scared cuz in that dream Him were leadin her father – the polygamous, polyamourous and polytheistic Thor Fruitmeat – towards her. It were sexual abuse condoned by Jah-Hee-Zeus Himself. Ginger had strayed too far from the path of Lord Szczmawg. So Jah-Hee-Zeus punished her by means of her daddy Thor Fruitmeat ..... who had his way with her .....*

THE TRAGIC OCCURRENCE AT TOPS SUPERMARKET

Ginger tended a garden of fantasy that were part Marshmallow Fluff, part used French fry grease splattered in yellow-lined parkin spaces near the dumpster behind the *Your Host* restaurant. Her had surrendered to depravity and her innocence were long forgotten. Exhaustion often forced her to pull herself long the dark roads of the night with her tongue. The muscles of her tongue had become very strong in this way. Locals feared her tongue as one would a weapon – it were known to be as powerful as that of a komodo dragon. When her were caught stealin the last pair of poor woman's Tinseltown sunglasses from the pharmacy down on Main Street of Boresaw, New York – her eyes turned mercury silver and her tongue shot out the front door – like a fearsome tentacle of a giant squid – to burn and sting insolent 11 year old boys that was doin wheelies outside. Them boys was thrown off they spider bikes with banana seats and then they was hit by cars ..... after which them flew high over the traffic circle comin into town ..... doin triple flips like Romanian gymnasts ….. then crashin head first through the windows of Tops supermarket. Them dangled there, bodies on the outside, heads on the inside. Them was goners …..

As them bled to death ….. emotionally disconnected cashiers come over to nonchalantly address them dyin boys ….. "Got yer bonus card?" them sneered. Then them cashiers turned savage, ripped off the heads of the boys, warned the customers via intercom to clear out if them valued they lives and engaged in a game of murder ball with the decapitated cabezas. Some of the more darin consumers, who happened to be in Tops at the time, emptied the shelves in spite of they fear – a golden opportunity had arisen in them moments of carnage that could not be ignored – them was hard times. Them cashiers laughed and laughed, but as them ultimately had need of a new thrill – them got in a huddle to plan they next move. Them waited, as if in a strange group meditation, for the dark to come. Then them dumped they uniforms into the laundry bin by the door of the manager's office. Then them lit up torches and marched out to the Center Road home of they universally despised field hockey coach, Boris Astromapolov. Him were a type that were always looked down upon by them uppity pipples of Smellicottville. Them girls was such a fearful sight as them passed through the village that the pious who witnessed they sinister march drew they blinds, turned off they lights and prayed to they proper monotheistic deity. Upon the girls' discovery of Boris Astromapolov engagin in sexual acts with his wife ..... them girls was way too turned on due to they youth and to the unexpected effects of this voyeuristic experience. And so them engaged in embarrassin and sometime tentative group masturbation. When them was done, them knew what them done were wrong and the entire pack were overcome with a deep burnin shame, especially due to they witnessin of that couple's amorousness. Them warn't too young to know what sexual love was. But them knew that them was still afraid of it and that them had been exposed to a reality from which them had been protected for all of they small town lives. So in they abyss of despair, them decided that life were a waste of time and there warn't no point in goin on .....

..... After tearin off the limbs of Boris Astromapolov and his wife as if them was a reincarnation of the Manson Family Girls ..... them set fire to the deceased couple's body parts in the living room of they house. Them poured more gasoline roun the first floor of the house and then them threw some lit matches on it before runnin outside to the front yard. Then them doused each other with gasoline, lit up some more matches and engaged in a ritualistic suicide pact. The sight of that thar house blowin up into a fiery explosion – along with that thar pack of girls in flames, fallin down in agony and staggerin afore they died – caused Henriette Hassenpfeffer to peer out of her kitchen window and raise an eyebrow while preparin a Blundt cake ..... "All on account of them self-immolatin girls – desserts can't be made proper no more! If only them girls was more like my Amazonian daughter Lula Bell! Then them would have been able to go onto achievin greatness in college and to have become high-powered executives in the burgeonin ethanol industry. Lula Bell is the macho queen of the Lower Dwellers in the Valley of Disillusionment! And I am right proud of her." ..... Then that too-sweet Blundt cake did fall, causin Mrs. Hassenpfeffer to curse a blue streak to the high heavens. Thereupon *stigmata* appeared on Henriette's palms. Blood then shot up from those wounds, horizontally from her eye sockets and upwards from the center of the ruined cake. The kitchen suddenly and inexplicably become hermetically sealed, the room filled up with blood and Mrs. Hassenpfeffer were drowned. Her were bein punished by the Wykkan gods fer havin witnessed a mystery that were both sacred and profane .....

BACK TO GINGER

One tongue-pullin post-rape-by-mutual-consent-night ..... Ginger seen eyes a-shinin bright Day-Glo green in the distance. Her were deep in the midst of a feral hallucination caused by havin nothin but the wrong kind of mens ..... *Bad mens is hot ..... them are like adult film pictures etched into my mind. I keeps them under lock and key in my fantasy chamber – where them comes and goes only as I please!* ..... her whispered to herself. Her face were swollen red and purple – some no good had come long and knocked her round. One night, after one too many Jenny Cream ales, her threw up at the feet of the local sheriff as them met at the edge of a cornfield (her didn't know when to stop). Him gave her a ride home although him regretted that him wouldn't be gettin no action that night. So him let her know forcefully that a raincheck were necessary in the near future, if her didn't want to be driven out of town. Or worse .....

Ginger's girlfriends at Aszczford Livelie Hallow High School wore too much makeup. Some of them was lookin like laidies that had already done too much. Them was constantly gossipin bout Ginger – her intrigued them ..... "Where her goin in the night?" ..... "Her on the Eden Corn Festival Preparation Committee?" ..... "Her waitin fer Santa Claus with a Great Punkin head?" ..... "Don't follow her nowhere. Her goin straight down the incinerator chute to damnation" ..... "Now let's stop all this bad talkin bout Ginger. How bout usns change our dirty underwear, pull on our sexy ass Sergio Valente jeans and head over to Pill Bar for some Michelobs?" ..... "Frig that. Let's hijack old man Conniver

Witherhyde's van, him are dead drunk right bout this time – and shoot up to Niagara Falls to smell chemical factory fumes by the gorge." ….. "Then usns can cruise back down to Kissin Bridge and toss aerosol cans into a bonfire in them piney woods!" ….. Then them giggled, high-fived each other and farted. Even if them didn't have nothin else, them relished they tradition of shared gas. Them had a lot of leftover methane built up from the frustration of havin to sit in school not knowin nothin. Either that or them was so incredibly anxious that they methane production were astronomical. That gas caused them to bond together as tightly as matriarchal wolves as them unknowinly contributed to global warmin. And in wintertime ….. what a relief it were to howl up towards the sky on a deep-freezin full moon snow-covered night.

Ginger lived with her maw and step-paw in a 1950's style one-story brick bungalow next to the Gowanda Drive-In. Them all spoke in the low-class heavily nasal accent of Western New York that emphasized flat A's. Rich people turned up they noses when them heard that accent as if powerful farts had been blown in they faces. The drive-in warn't showin movies no more. It were an elephant's graveyard of dysfunctional nightmares. It were a big vacant lot sprinkled with broken glass, soda pop cans, rusty trashcans and doll parts ….. with dandelions, Queen Anne's Lace and Indian Paintbrushes growin up through cracks in the cement. Durin most evenins, Ginger's maw, Francine Kafka, could be found loungin on the tan-colored couch in the TV light, her bare feet restin on the dirty aquamarine polyester shag carpet. Ginger also had a little brother named Rusty who were very shy, serial-killer smart, didn't say nearly nothin and lived in a fantasy world. One not so fine night, Francine put her jug of Paul Masson brandy down and wailed up to Ginger ….. "Turn that goddam punk rock down!" ….. Ginger had only put it on to cover Old Man Witherhyde's grunts of satisfaction when her gave him a blowjob. Him would crawl up a rope confiscated from an old tire swing to Ginger's window and supply her with an allowance fer services rendered. When spry Old Man Witherhyde climbed back out of the window after them was done, Ginger turned off her bad-girl music and got back to bein absorbed in her paperback copy of *Szczmawgwhore(ts): A Pornographick Bitch-Story*.

Next Sunday, it were a fine Cattaraugus county mornin. Ginger (not never havin been no church-goer) awoke in a room of the Pink Fountain Motor Court in Batavia, New York with a shaft of sunlight fallin across her tattooed ass. Her had spent the night undergoin a spiritual conversion with her bare calves wrapped around the rim of the Porcelain God. Her enjoyed the feelin of the cold tiles and toilet on her bare skin. Her wondered what schemes of manipulation her would have to employ to get the money for her genital piercin from her maw Francine. Ginger would have to take a bus all the way to Buffalo to get that – maybe even to Toronto, Kanader – where ungodly Commonwealth influences floated around like pagan spirits, settllin down into the minds of freaks starin outta the windows of streetcars that was crossin town ….. "Maw's makin good money now down at the Fisher Price toy factory. I seen her pay stub so I know her is right near rich." ….. Father Elizabeth Branigan, who Ginger worshipped as bein somethin more satisfyin than all the rest of her recent tricks, were shavin her poossy as the repression of the church were jes too much for him. Ginger loathed him – but that's how it were with all mens and that were the price her paid for gettin action. In short – her had never been choosy. To cope with the present situation, yet another in a string of ugly, humiliatin realities ..... her migrated in her mind to Salinas, California by means of Porn Key physio-animation ..... because the air were more dry there in Cali and it were full of cheap motels whose violent customers trashed the rooms screamin in the night ..... an ambience that Ginger done found right pleasin .....

Ginger and Father Elizabeth Branigan (or "Devil Horns" as him were known in them parts) had been to an orgy the night before in a gas station bathroom across from a Pink Catawba vineyard in Chautauqua County. Thus them were lookin worse for the wear. Devil Horns were now applyin his David Bowie-style makeup (him also idolized the David Lee Roth-esque drag queen psycho-killer of *Silence of the Lambs*) ..... right pleasin Ginger whose white trash sexual sophistication had been acquired through environmental conditionin. And her did fiercely covet that quality. Devil Horns said the Lord Szczmawg Prayer and placed his face in Ginger's gaszcz – sinful behavior for which him would later atone – bein that him were a double-agent practitioner of monotheism. While him were down there ….. him fantasized bout some of his favorite mens. Him preferred a more natural look, like them provincial Europeans with non-gym-toned bodies.

Ginger yawned, completely bored. Her sensibility had been dulled by the soulless inhumanity of constant unsexy sex. "Is ityergirly time Ginger?" Devil Horns sneered in his lovin priestly way (among the seminarians – him had been known as "George Sanders"). As payback, Ginger kicked damn Devil Horns in the balls and his hyena-banshee yowls was heard all the way cross the world in Morewhore ….. "How you feel now, Monsignor Bitch-Ass Branigan? Now you can go be like my platonic friend Djzheemi Sparks, the prude son of squares that live up in that fancy mansion on Mill Road Hill. Them Sparks boys got eyes like does! THEY SO SOFT! ….. All I know is that Djzheemi Sparks is spoiled rotten and for that reason alone ….. I will jealously and heartlessly harass him and his kind.

Underneath that asexual timidity of Djzheemi Sparks lurks a lecherous satyr yearnin to break free from his moralistic prison. I will defile him and bring him face to face with my high-velocity brute reality" .....

Fer Devil Horns, Ginger bored were an aphrodisiac and him took Polaroids of her lookin like that. "I like that blank expression on yer face like you got yer brains all fucked out. Makes me wanna see you in a snuff film wearin a rubber mask with no eye holes or nose holes. Mouth hole only Ginger ..... mouth hole only. Imagine bein in a forest of faceless cocks. Now wouldn't that be near close to paradise? Makes me wish you were all lobotomized like that Francine Farmer. Maybe you don't know it yet ..... but there's a future for you in German Shit Porn – you sassy brassy lady ....."

As Devil Horns clicked away, Ginger surrendered to the fantasy, pretendin her were a character in a Tawdry Fartburn movie with way too much time and money on her hands. Her squeezed her breasts with her vicious red-door-painted-black fingernails and howled like a werewoolf. Then her laughed in a way so wicked that it were guaranteed to make any

Honor Society student tremble with terror. Blushin in the euphoria of the excitement and shame of Ginger's expressiveness ..... Devils Horns ran down to St. Lucille del Malocchio's parish. A bake sale were in progress in the shuffleboard floor basement ..... but him were unobserved as him went upstairs to the chapel ..... where him pulled down his pants and plopped his bare ass into the baptismal font. Him crapped enthusiastically in that thar font. And when him were done, him made joyful cooin baby sounds that warn't never allowed in his childhood.

FRANCINE KAFKA

Francine Kafka took a break from the Paul Masson brandy and opened her mouth as wide as a wind tunnel. With her cheeks blowed up and gums showin, her called to her daughter ..... "Come and get it! Maw done made Ginger's favorite! Defecation Parfait!" When Ginger done heard Maw's dinner call, her ears went woolven and her let out a supersonic wail ..... "Shoot brown rockets out yer waste hole and straight into my facial orifice, Maw Kettle!"

her blasted. Maw's dinner call made her so excited that it were as if Quasimodo himself were ringin his big iron Notrey Dammy church bells inside her vagina ….. "There's always more brown where that come from!" Francine hollered back. "You been such a sweet little ho this year – that next December 25th after Santa Claus brush burns his boner comin down the chimney – he'll find a note by the milk and cookies directin him right up to yer room – to treat you to a ravishin! I gets such a feelin of power envisionin yer rape by Santa Claus!" ….. "I can't wait Maw! I'll go temporarily celibate fer that roly-poly red-cheeked bundle of joy!"

ROAD TRIP TO CALI

Ginger and Devil Horns took off on a trip to Southern Cali-Forn-Eye-Ay where them rode down twisty creepy roads in his fire-engine red Camaro. Them snaked through them thar barren hills of the Suede Tan Mountains on the way to a tranquil picnickin spot between Blood Gush Lake and the gurglin source of Mud Slide Crik. Then them pulled over to the side of the road and stopped for a breath of fresh air in the cool desert evenin. Also Devil Horns needed to step outside to soothe his burnin hemorrhoids with Amelia Dickersin witch hazel (this involved cleanin his ass crack thoroughly). Thar warn't no kind uh recognizabibble veggietation, as far as the eye could see, fer a person accustomed to seein plant life from wetter climes. It were a new world where blood had replaced water. Many thirsted in this purgatory. Legend has it that there were a local portal in the area leadin to the Orphic Underworld. But in real world terms – that thar crik were full of industrial oil, detergent and birds that done died from the West Nile virus. The hot-blooded waters of this meta-blue sky country inspired Devil Horns in the pursuit of his vulgar earthly needs. Him bellowed to his Wykkan gods and grunted as him pushed out brown. Him had growed up like a weed in the earthquake-cracked sidewalk outside a state mental hospital – survivin wherever and however it can. Him were like an anaerobic organism that lived on top of boilin black sulfurous jets at the bottom of the deepest places in the ocean. In his moments of greatest pain, Devil Horns imagined all of the nastiness of his disgustin life – and all of the rest of the world – bein washed away by purifyin waters like done happened in the tale of Noah's Ark …..

Meanwhile back in the Camaro – Devil Horns sat in the driver's seat with the door open. Him were contemplatin the hypocritical manifestation of the Anti-Christ in his pants and didn't care bout nothin else at that moment – least of all the sermon he'd be preachin the next day at Saint Gargoyles Congregation of Wayward Blasphemy in nearby Santa Maria [him were substitutin for the latest preacher to have been struck down by Holy Snake Venom]. In his secular downtime, Devil Horns hungered for a wide range of types ….. *incested womanly teenagers like Ginger; buxom barmaids from late 17th century Salem, Massachusetts; altar boys in red and white vestments, hyper-effeminate tattooed muscle boys, alpha males masqueradin as fine upstandin citizens in uniforms appropriate to they respective professions (be they sheriff, policeman, or construction worker)* ….. The sky glowed orange-rose-purple and the light of the desert exo-suburbs twinkled in the distance. Them had built a cracklin fire by the shore of the crik and had turned off the headlights to better enjoy the night skies. Ginger had fallen asleep, exhausted by her decadent cravins and disturbin fantasies. Devil Horns examined a copy of Wurkgurl by flashlight in loo of studyin a map of the area. Owls and coyotes hooted and howled, bats flew from caves and rattlesnakes that was too close for comfort swallowed kangaroo rats whole as the sky went from violet to indigo .....

Once durin a rare uncomforbibble moment of reflection, Ginger had confessed to Devil Horns ..... *Mommer told me that usns had puritanical ancestors that come over on that Mayflower ship ..... that them was a pipple so full of hot sexy fire that them had to hide it all inside and act like them was right respecabibble! Somehow them squandered they fortunes over the years through the compulsive channelin of they shameful, taboo desires ..... and that's how usns ended up in the trailer park by the Winsome Witchpot Restaurant on Route 77 .....* As Ginger slept in the front seat of the Camaro, her dreamt about a book that her had tried to read in 9th grade, *Great Expectations*, that had bored her awful. In this dream ..... Miss Havisham were masturbatin furiously as her grabbed a hunk of rat-infested weddin cake and shoved it down Ginger's throat. But Ginger fought back hard with fearsome koont poonches to the great surprise of that dastardly dayme ..... her telekineticized Miss Havisham's bony ass ..... slammin her into window boards that blocked out the sunlight ..... fillin the back side of that bitter old bitch ass bitch with splinters and rusty screws. Then the whole rundown 19th century Victorian mansion split apart and were flooded with the muddy waters of a tsunami ..... Ginger were swept out of Miss Havisham's life-negatin chamber and onto a Bourbon Street balcony where her clung for dear life ..... prayin to her Wykkan majesties fer salvation ...... then her watched Miss Havisham turn blue, swell up to the size of a giant exercise ball ..... with her eyes poppin out of her head ..... and then explode ..... to be washed away in them wretched flood waters .....

A few hours later, Ginger awoke with a start and looked at Devil Horns with dumbfounded amazement. Her tried to explain her dream, but her description emerged instead in a kind of Shakespearian English ..... *Twere but a fiendish synchronicitie. Wouldst that thou proferred upon me a goblet of Ganymede wine. Wherein I should be stood in good stead and no longer would the torment of these sexy yet soulless nights assail my person with such vehemence …..*

BACK FROM CALI

Back in Western New York after her West Coast excursion, Ginger thunk of nothin as her passed out droolin on her undone homework in Mr. Boccaccio's chemistry class. Her dreamt of orgies with her male schoolteachers in the dark room where pictures was developed fer the upcomin yearbook. Durin the day, them role models took on attitudes of moral superiority. But in Ginger's subconscious them teachers appeared as illiterate sex zoombies moanin ….. *find the orifices* ….. with they pants pulled down roun they ankles and they eyes rolled up into the backs of they heads …..

Later that night, right roun bout twilight time – Ginger's maw howled out like a coal miner ….. "Girl we got caramel fer caramel-coated apples boilin in a black cast-iron Wykkan cauldron out by the barn fer orange-black Halloween time!" Ginger hollered back ..... "You done made Shitfruit Pie Maw? Oh please say yes! I ain't never tasted no other Shitfruit Pie like yers!" ..... The rain had been abundant that late winter and the surroundin hills was covered with the sphincter-shaped blooms of the Shit Flower Tree. Springtime's blessins, curses, assets and liabilities was all too much for Ginger. Springtime reminded her that her had entered the world of adult sexuality way too soon without havin had no kinda proper instruction as to how it should be navigated. So Ginger held on real tight to whatever scraps of innocence her were aware of ..... like her memory of bein a 5 year-old girl playin grownup with feets and a body too small for Francine Kafka's heels and dresses .....

FRANCINE KAFKA

Francine Kafka

In the town of Blowdy, in the flattest part of Kansas, many of its residents was frighteninly fair-skinned. Them was referred to as The Pale Ones. And even on the most breathtaking late afternoon summer days, a spectre of menace loomed over the town. Old Man Witherhyde inevitably greeted visitors – who rolled slowly through the village, peerin out of they car windows – with the followin recitation ….. "Don't matter when you relocate yerself to Blowdy ….. you won't be leavin til the Carnival Barker-Undertaker tips his top hat to you and throws you down into yer freshly prepared grave. Unless you prefer to be consumed by one of our curiously translucent inhabitants who lurk in abandoned buildings with grotesque smiles and a cold-blooded gleam in they eyes. In fact, where they should have two eyes ..... they got two mouths. And where they should have a mouth ..... they got one eye. Everthin's all mixed up, upside-down and backwards in Blowdy. Consider that a warnin." At the end of his speech, Old Man Witherhyde would dance a wild jig ..... screechin and wailin in a paranormal trance .....

Some visitors that didn't know any better got it in they minds that them could live in Blowdy without fear. But usually them was overwhelmed by a feelin of heaviness. All the Pale Ones had to do were to point at they victim, with both arms extended, while lightly tappin the tips of they fingers together. This worked like a form of hypnotism ..... the Pale Ones would stare at they target like a lionesse that seduces in order to kill. It were like bein smacked on the back of the neck with a shovel so hard that the poor unfortunate's eyes was crossed and the wind were knocked out of them. And to top it all off ..... whoever were on the receivin end of this brute force were sent directly down to the pitch black circles of an Orphic Underworld that were far beyond anythin that Dantey Ali-Geary had ever imagined.

Although the village itself appeared to be charmin, the outskirts of Blowdy was an industrial wasteland where ghostly buildins exploded into flames and corrodin garbage cans was filled with the blood of they victims. Directly beneath the open fields on the periphery of town were a kingdom of komodo dragons like nothin that had been seen since the time of Jah-Hee-Zeus. That thar komodo dragon kingdom were a veritable mine field and one were guaranteed to lose at least a foot or a leg – if one had the misfortune of crossin over it. Them komodo critters stuck they heads up out of the holes of they burrows, snappin they jaws like alligators. And them amputated limbs of them unfortunates made nature's garden grow up jes that much brighter. But the biggest appetites of all belonged to the castratin Venus flytraps. When supplies of male genitalia was scarce, them Venus flytraps survived by devourin bees. Which resulted in makin honey a precious commodity in the area ….. *"Them Venus flytrappers done ate all the bees!"* ….. *the Pale Ones would exclaim* ….. The sky-high price of honey made them Blowdyites fear that them wouldn't have enough reserves left for the upcomin Black–Indigo-Violet Friday, a local holiday.

The town directly west of Blowdy – Sassafras – warn't near so sinister. Francine Kafka were a proud resident of Sassafrass. Her liked hitchin at night on dark country roads in the area as well as cussin out drivers that warn't givin no rides. There were always that odd chance that her would end up chopped up in the trunk of some psycho's car and then dumped into a ditch. But her kept that thought still in a dark corner of her mind like a solitary spiritual candle. Francine made splatter paintins to blow off steam. And beyond that, her also enjoyed defacin public property with buckets of house paint. Her had recently hurled paint up onto a billboard advertisin Barbyzonya Solar-Wind, Goddess of Hyperventilation and Empress of Neglected Southern Gothic Traumas, in her latest film ….. Ye Temple of The Deitie of Ye Olde Englyshe Leather.

One day, Francine woke up and thought to herself ….. *I don't want to be no goddam coke dealer no more. I'm tired of dangerous predators prowlin outside my trailer 24-7. I will pray to the Hawk-Headed*

Goddess for guidance. She will enlighten me as to how I can get me a more satisfyin career ….. When Francine found out that "A Well-Renowned Leader of the Evilangelists" would be speakin at a local university, she said to herself ….. Somethin must be done to stop this abomination ….. somehow I'll ensnare him ….. I'll dance on his bare butt cheeks sportin killer spike heels by the magical glow of a roarin fire. Him will be hypnotized and then bathed in the blood of abortions in a heart-shaped Jacuzzi transported from a romantic Rocky Mountain getaway. Then him will be stunned and anaesthetized and samples will be taken from his organs to be used fer stem cell research by local scientists. Them Evilangelists will be protestin outside. Even if I try my best to keep the whole thing covert ….. them'll find out. Them always got they ears to the groun lookin to dig up dirt! Well they can scream theyselves hoarse ….. Ah revenge is sweet! I know that I can make this happen. I no longer regret spendin a heap of time in the self-help section of Borders. By followin my bliss, I now know such serenity ….. as if the national debt of Amurycka Profunda had been cancelled in an instant …..

Francine giggled at the cheap Satanick vocal-effects used for the flamin faggot Persian king Xerxes in *300* ….. *It were a highly visual film, lackin in content but givin good form. A form that I felt intrigued by. And who wouldn't be titillated by them leather-constrained bulges of them warriors? Did such Krissuhfuh Street Kräftsmanship really exist back in them polytheistick days? I'm ashamed to admit that it were difficult to go to church on Sunday after watchin that movie. In antiquated times, things was more liberal than now. But then them early Christians come along and set things right with they willinness to die fer they faith. And Maya Hiyuh Powuh knows this had to happen because they was probably some AIDS-like disease goin roun that usns don't have no records of no more ….. because all them had was chisels and stones and it took too much time fer they secretaries to take all of that information down …..*

….. I'm right steamed about how much movies cost these days ….. specially the ones that don't speak to the hypocrisy of small-town Amurycka Profundan values. I'm gonna write that Snivelly McClintock and tell her that the price of admission to the Circus Maximus

is jes too damn high. Last night, I were watchin that movie Gilbert Grape on the DVD. Gilbert Grape is my Casablanca. It's like lookin in a mirror that shows my life back to me. I always want to shoot myself whenever I watch it. Yes I am a romantic ..... but I am also dealin with a deep depression. I tried everthin ..... therapy, anti-depressants, Twelve Step programs. I took what worked for me and I left the rest! So now when hopelessness beckons, I jes raise up my hands to the sky and say hello to my girlfriend Maya Hiyuh Powuh. Whenever I can't see no silver linin in no cloud ..... I eat a devil's food chocolate sheet cake and then it's like bluebirds be singin on the first day of spring. When I inhale that sheet cake like Jobba the Koont ..... life be good .....

Francine's son Rusty won the spellin bee fer the Sassafrass Middle School 7th grade class. Which made her very happy ..... "Him's mommy's number one little bitch" ..... her liked to say. Rusty's English teacher – Madam Pentacostya Koontwych – had recommended him fer a short story contest as well. Her had recently announced the names of the three prospective entrants in the competition durin a school assembly. Madam Koontwych were an overqualified PhD that entertained local businessmen in mid-grade motels. Her didn't find out til the last minute that the name of Rusty's story were *Gluteus Maximus: An Exhibitionistic Exploration of Friendship between Males*. A controversial title of that nature could result in the suspension of Rusty. But Madam Koontwych announced the title anyways – her were lookin for some drama. Her wanted to sabotage Rusty – as her were disillusioned with her sordid extra-curricular activities. Someone would have to pay – and in Rusty her had found the weakest link of the chain. Her would take Rusty down with her sinkin ship. Her knew that painfully shy Rusty wouldn't fight back. Most of the students was confused by the title of Rusty's story. But them was soon informed of its meanin by the more darin among them. Once word of the title of Rusty's story started circulatin among the student body – Rusty were slammed into lockers fer weeks afterward. Francine grounded him and kept him in virtual seclusion fer the followin month, while his latent homosexuality were bein evaluated by the school psychiatrist. Francine had the windows of Rusty's bedroom painted black and when that were done, she locked him in. If him dared to scratch off the paint ….. him would be spanked with a shovel. Francine addressed him through his bedroom door fiercely ….. *So now it'll be as dark in yer room as it is in them assholes you been dreamin bout where the sun don't never shine. What the hell you thinkin ….. that some smelly brown rectum's yer idea of paradise? Maybe I'm jumpin the gun ….. but I sure hope youse gonna make use of condoms and enemas in yer adult life. There's a fearful amount of diseases associated with the ass. And one can't go roun indiscriminately offerin one's backside lovehole to ever stranger as if him were the Royal Blue Prince. Furthermore, yer silence will be mighty appreciated, as it will prevent me from executin continued abuse upon yer person* ….. She then left him to his insomnia that were caused by a fear of gym days due to covert sexual attractions to boys in the showers …..

That night Rusty had a dream ….. *Him were in the breakfast room of an over-rated stuck up 3 star hotel in Paris, France ….. surrounded by morose portly couples gnawin on French bread. Except Rusty warn't* seated at no table. Him were sittin in a sandbox that were filled with dirt ….. dressed in a diaper and suckin on a passafire. Then him were eatin somethin ….. at first, him thought it were a chocolate croissant ….. but it turned out to be a shit-prune-mud croissant. Suddenly a big fat Amurycka Profundan wuhmyn named Doris Krullermunch appeared ….. draggin her gigantic ass behind her. Her couldn't make it through the entranceway ….. her ass were jes too damn big. The waitress spoke to Doris in Parisian-accented English ….. I am so sorry meez but your boat-um eez too beeg for theez breakfast room ….. Doris responded by beggin pathetically fer somethin to eat ….. Jes one little hard-boiled egg! I'm practically starvin! I haven't eaten fer 8 hours! But the waitress refused and all of the clients in the breakfast room started laughin at Doris. The waitress wanted a few laughs too ….. so her started shovin dirt from the sandbox into her mouth while jumpin up and down screamin ….. I am a sheet-eating whore! Doris dissolved into a pool of tears ….. then turned into a pan of bacon and eggs fryin ….. this made the guests convulse even more. Then Doris transformed herself into a cloud of purple gas (Rusty's subconscious sure liked its pretty colors!). But the purple gas that once were Doris Krullermunch were so volatile ..... that when the laughin waitress struck a match to light a sterno can on the buffet table ..... her burst into flames along with everone else in the room. The resultin fire consumed the rest of the hotel. There was no survivors and the buildin were demolished to make way for a McDonalds that featured pre-fabricated chocolate croissants on the menu .....

BOBBY CHUSHINGURA

Bobby Chushingura

Bobby Chushingura had placed a curse on himself by strangling his childhood sweetheart, Alison Sh*tbox, to death during a ritual of erotic asphyxiation. Bobby had ingeniously made the murder look like a drug overdose-suicide. He had slipped sedatives into Alison's beer before she was murdered. She was found hanging from the railing of the second-floor landing of the Sh*tbox' family home. Bobby had grown up on the wrong side of the tracks of a rural-suburban Rust Belt town populated by wealthy equestrian enthusiasts who were only as sick as their secrets. As a child, Bobby would hold his buddies by their ankles from the neighbor's tree house, frightening them out of their wits, before pulling them back up and telling them ominously ..... *I was just kidding*

..... The question his fellow classmates usually asked themselves when they saw him walking towards them in the hallway was this ..... *What isn't wrong with Bobby Chushingura?* Bobby screamed at his teachers, received failing grades and sniffed glue. He jabbed his fellow students with chisels in shop class, dropped dumbbells on their toes in the weight room and was known to fill the high school swimming pool with massive quantities of Jell-O. In Boby's hands, a pink flamingo garden ornament became a lethal weapon. And yet he could convince any of the local mental health professionals that each of the offenses he had committed upon his peers had happened by accident and that he was entirely sane.

Bobby often bragged about his violent conquests to his classmates as they waited for the school bus in the morning ..... *Mother once advised me to seek out victims and attack them with the force of a vampire. I am intuitive. I am aware of the blurry line that divides art and criminality. Before I could speak, I knew that NIGHT + NIGHT = DOUBLE DARK = DOUBLE BLACK; therefore: NIGHT + NIGHT = DOUBLE BLACK. Who said I wasn't any good at math? And SATs are bullshit! I'll ace a Rorschach test any day!* ..... One evening after a particularly bitter encounter with his guidance counselor, Konrad Kraftwerk, who had suggested to Bobby that he would make a great auto mechanic since he wouldn't have to work with people – Bobby started a huge bonfire on the high school football field where he burned every dirty gym outfit that he could find in both the girls' and the boys' locker rooms.

One day, Bobby was at the house of a friend – Sasha Sh*tbox, the brother of the late Alison Sh*tbox. Mr. and Mrs. Sh*tbox were Evilangelists who had forgiven Bobby for murdering their daughter Alison though constant prayer to Jah-Hee-Zeus. They greeted Bobby kindly at the door, thinking that they could charm him by playing selections from *Andy William's Greatest Hits* on their stereo system. But how naïve they were! Bobby saw through their futile attempt at manipulation and in a show of appreciation, he smashed up the Sh*tbox' stereo with a crowbar [Bobby always knew where to find the tools]. The Sh*tboxes and their son Sasha were then bound and gagged – and subsequently tossed into the gigantic piranha-filled aquarium in the living room – where they were then devoured in a bloody feeding-frenzy. Everyone was expendable in Bobby's universe. And of course, Bobby got away with it. He was an immaculate perfectionist – he knew how to wrap up a body in plastic – dead or alive. Forensics experts found some circumstancial evidence at the scene of the crime that ultimately became irrelevant ..... as what always saved Bobby was his complete lack of conscience. He loved to lie and he never broke a sweat in doing so. And he felt no compulsion to confess.

Bobby couldn't remember a time when the killing blood did not rise up within him upon the slightest provocation. Aggression, adrenalin, deviance, hostility and pain were his only friends. A smile from that rare peer that said ..... *I'd like to get to know you* ..... sent him through the roof. Bobby's shop teacher, Horace "Whore-Ass" Snufflelump, encouraged him to pursue a glass-blowing career – in a vain attempt to get Bobby back on his good side – after Bobby had threatened to burn out Snufflelump's eyes with sulfuric acid. Horace sang Bobby's praises like a beatnik (Mr. Snufflelump had no idea just how hip he truly was).

Snuffleump praised Bobby sycophantically via the following recitation ..... as if he was Jack Kerouac doing spoken-word stream of consciousness poetry in a late 1950s black and white French film accompanied by a jazzy soundtrack ..... HOT, MOLTEN, SCORCHING! THAT'S BOBBY! BLOW BOBBY, BLOW BOBBY, BLOW BLOW BLOW! .....

Mr. Snufflelump, who everyone had thought was a pillar of the community, was later fired for soliciting tweenage boys in the locker room of the middle school gymnasium. Horace's wife, Svetlana, was furious when she found out. The very next day, she drugged him and then castrated him with garden shears (as if she was channeling Bobby Chushingura). Considering this to have been sufficient punishment, she left him in the SUV in the driveway and ran to turn off the smoke alarm (she was always cooking to beat the band even though she resented the hell out of it). Miracuously and in spite of his condition, Snufflelump managed to start up the SUV, back it out of the driveway and get the hell out of there. It started raining heavily soon after his escape ..... causing Snufflelump to swerve, fly over the railing at the side of the road and end up at the bottom of a deep ravine. His vehicle became a death trap. Upon its final impact, the SUV exploded into flames and Mr. Snufflelump then burnt to death (fortunately he was barely conscious at the time). It was the Curse of Bobby Chushingura ….. anyone who sent any kind of positive vibrations in Bobby's direction was sure to feel the eventual boomerang effect of Bobby's Anti-Karma Chameleon Old Black Magic.

Year later, Bobby became a professional embezzler, international fugitive and expert in all types of subterfuge. He relished the climate of fear fostered by the geopolitical atmosphere of the new millennium. Somehow Bobby was able to keep his negative emotions under control. Although those emotions often propelled him into a panic – the mask of his serial-killer charm remained securely in place. He struggled against everything within him that was appropriate, palatable, right-sized and civilized. A bottle of duty-free cognac and a variety of downers helped him to sleep off the jet lag in various decadent cities around the world. He secretly hoped that a suicide bomber would blow up his favorite sex club, as he had been unable to extract himself from his love-hate relationship with that netherworld – from that pleasure-pain continuum – that was one of his many torments.

Bobby's parents, Woofraymo and Warbullina Chushingura, stated that they were proud of him – although they had no idea where he had ended up after leaving home at the age of 18. They had not heard a word from him since. Then one day, they were informed that he had drowned in a tsunami in Southeast Asia. His badly decomposed body was returned to them and they promptly cremated it without a tear – as they were monsters themselves. As his mother Warbullina spoke about Bobby at the memorial, it became obvious to the few people in attendance that she was clearly delusional ….. *Bobby's in paradise now….. him's in an afterworld that combines the worst aspects of some of the world's wildest port cities – New Orleans, Amsterdam, Bangkok. Him speak the Frenchy French now in that Orphic Underworld Dantey Ali-Geary place where all of them deviants and perverts go. Him warn't never no good at book learnin ….. but that don't mean that him couldn't learn what him had to ….. to live wherever him wanted to on the Blue Green Planet. It warn't edge-uh-macation that done helped him to become who him were. It were discipline. When him were a boy ….. him got his ass beat ever lovin day by my hubbin ….. with a two-by-four in the hayloft of Amurycka Profunda's last barn ….. that were coincidentally right next door to our purty little one-story bungalow. Y'all can see how my hubbin Woofraymo got jes one eye after Bobby got mad after one of them whippins and burned it out with a blowtorch. But Woofraymo knew it were worth it. Them beatins made Bobby right responsabibble …..*

THE REVENGE OF ALISON SH*TBOX

THE REVENGE OF ALISON SH*TBOX

"I SEE YOU DOWN THERE IN HELL, ABOMINABLE, NEFARIOUS BOBBY CHUSHINGURA, YOU'LL PAY FOREVER FOR WHAT YOU DID, YOU'LL DIE OF A THOUSAND ELECTROCUTIONS, OF A THOUSAND LETHAL INJECTIONS! YOU'RE JUST LUCKY THIS HAPPENED TO YOU IN AMURYCKA PROFUNDA! BECAUSE OTHERWISE YOU WOULD HAVE BEEN STRUNG UP IN A NOOSE OR HAVE HAD YOUR HEAD CHOPPED OFF! YOU'RE A ROTTEN SNAKE GNAWING AT THE ROOTS OF YGGDRASIL, HYPONOTIZING ALL OF YO LADIES LIKE THE SOCIOPATH THAT YOU ARE! I'M LOOKING AT YOU WITH MY NOSE SMASHED UP FLAT ON THE SIDE OF THIS PIRAHNA-FISH TANK! I CAN'T SEE HARDLY ANYTHING BECAUSE IT'S

ALL FILLED UP WITH BLOOD! THOSE PIRAHNAS ARE STILL TRYING TO BITE OFF MY NOSE!

BUT THE AFTERLIFE LOOKS REAL NICE UP HERE – EVEN THOUGH I CAN'T GET TO IT YET! I'M PRETTY SURE I'M IN THE RIGHT PLACE. MY FIRST IMPRESSION IS THAT THIS IS MUCH MORE LIKE THE STEREOTYPICAL 'IT'S A WONDERFUL LIFE'-STYLE PEARLY GATES THAN THE LURID RED INFERNO OF HIERONYMOUS BOSCH. [THAT'S WHERE YOU ARE, BOBBY C.!] AND I'M SO GLAD! IT'S LIKE THE COVER OF THE WATCHTOWER UP HERE. WHATEVER ELSE THOSE PEOPLE GOT WRONG – THEY GOT THIS RIGHT! IT'S LIKE THE CAMPUS OF ORAL ROBERTS UNIVERSITY WITH BLUE SKIES AND BIRDS CHIRPING AND FAUX-IVY-LEAGUE-STYLE ARCHITECTURE! FRANKLY I'M HOPING THERE WILL BE MORE OF A DRUIDYCK SPIRITUALITY HERE THAN THAT OF MONOTHEISM. MAYBE I'M IN VALHAHA – OH I DO HOPE IT'S TRUE! ALTHOUGH IN NORSE MYTHOLOGY, THE DOPPELGÄNGER IS NEARLY ALWAYS UNDERSTOOD TO BE AN EVIL SPIRIT – IT IS IN FACT A CHILLING PREMONITION OF THE SHADOW OF DEATH. WERE YOU MY DOPPELGÄNGER, BOBBY CHUSHINGURA? WAS THAT MY DESTINY? IS THAT WHY I HAD TO LEAVE THE BLUE GREEN PLANET IN THE

SPRINGTIME OF MY LIFE? TOO LATE TO WORRY ABOUT THAT NOW, BOBBY. OUR DOPPELGÄNGERS HAVE DONE THEIR WORK …..

BUT DON'T LET ANY OF THIS GET YOU DOWN! EVEN IF SOMETIMES I BEHAVE LIKE A VICIOUS, GROWLING WOUNDED ANIMAL WHO'S BEEN BACKED UP INTO A CORNER – I'VE ALWAYS BEEN AN "UP, UP WITH PEOPLE", "UP UP AND AWAY IN MY BEAUTIFUL BALLOON", "I'D LIKE TO TEACH THE WORLD TO SING" KIND OF OPTIMIST. AND I ALWAYS WANT YOU TO REMEMBER ME THAT WAY! I SEE SOME VERY HAPPY PEOPLE NEARBY AND THEY'RE HAVING A VEGAN BARBECUE WITH TOFU, TEMPEH, PORTOBELLO MUSHROOMS, GRILLED VEGETABLES AND EVEN COLD SESAME NOODLES AS A SIDE DISH. WHEREAS ALL THE CARNIVORES ARE DOWN THERE IN THE NINTH CIRCLE OF HELL WITH YOU! RIGHT MR. C.?

BUT I MUST BE IN SOME KIND OF PURGATORY BECAUSE I HAVEN'T SPOKEN TO ANYONE SINCE I ARRIVED HERE. THERE MUST BE A DIFFERENT CONFIGURATION OF TIME GOING ON IN THIS PLACE. NEEDLESS TO SAY – IF THIS IS THE GREEN ROOM FOR MY REINCARNATION – I LIKE IT! I HOPE I NO LONGER HAVE BODILY

NEEDS, I HOPE THERE'S NO MORE ACID REFLUX, AND MOST OF ALL I HOPE THERE'S NO NEED FOR COLON CLEANSERS. ALTHOUGH I'M AWFULLY CRAMPED IN HERE! I FEEL LIKE MY HEAD HAS BEEN TIED UP TO MY FEET! I FEEL LIKE ALL OF MY APPENDAGES HAVE BEEN HANDCUFFED TO EACH OTHER ....."

Back on the Blue Green Planet ..... the casket of Alison Sh*tbox was being lowered into the ground. The sky was full of dark gray clouds and the wind had picked up, giving everyone a chill. All of the attendees were devastated over this senseless loss of life. So what if Alison had been so far from being a model citizen? So what if she had been a slut, a delinquent and a hater who showed up to school every day drunk? Death never plays fair. Everyone deserves a second chance – even those existentialists who transcend their fears and jump at opportunities as if it was second nature. The guests at the funeral were of the tough working-class type – bartenders, secretaries, cops, hairdressers, tattoo artists, auto mechanics and gun shop owners. And the crowd was mostly men – practically all of the women in town had felt threatened by Alison Sh*tbox. On the other hand, all of those women who were present at the solemnities could readily put themselves into the shoes of Alison Sh*tbox. And they hoped that Bobby Chushingura was burning in hell for what he had done .....

EUPHEMIA STATISTYKA

A preppy, upper-middle class girl from an adjacent county had shown up at Alison's funeral. She was wearing a kelly green monogram sweater, chocolate brown corduroys and she considered herself to be above this scenario. She was there to do research about "life on the other side of the tracks". Her name was Euphemia Statistyka and she had stereotyped Alison Sh*tbox as white trash, solely because she had spelled her name "Alison" with one L ..... "Alison would never be accepted by the status-seekers of those towns nearby where I live on the far eastern end of Long Guile-Land. Anyone knows that living in Middl Earf Hampton is MAKING IT" ..... Euphemia said under her breath. Euphemia was a stay-in-the-lines type of aspiring graphic artist for whom Abstract Expressionism – an art form that was already at least sixty years old – was still radical and wholly incomprehensible. Euphemia was therefore the perfect choice for editor of the Middl Earf Hampton High School yearbook. Still, as derivative as she was, she fancied herself to be a colorist ….. "On clear-blue-sky autumn days, I long to immerse myself in the brilliant hues of the foliage of the Delaware Water Gap. It's the earth colors that I'm particularly drawn to ….. the brick reds, the suede yellow-tans, the rusty brown oranges ….. the fecund green of the last gasp of summer that hangs on until Old Man Winter curls up his long, spindly, sinister fingers into the ball of a fist and smashes all of the fragile brown leaf pre-humus into the compost of the elaborate suburban gardens of tacky social-climbing families ….. who then enrich that compost even further by nourishing it with coffee grounds, egg shells and banana peels ….."

….. "I remember natural beauty of this kind while visiting my aunt Martyra in suburban Ohio ….. driving down a lovely road in a wooded area that featured some of the most expensive homes in the Columbus area. I still didn't have my driver's license ….. I was in the back seat of the car with my brother. My father drove and my mother sat next to him. We were driving through a small ravine filled with the entangled vines of early spring's still-hibernating vegetation. There were undeveloped lots along the brown-water creek that was polluted with phosphates, industrial waste and drugs used for animal-testing. Back in Gowanda (where I had spent my early childhood before our family moved to Middl Earf Hampton and became *nouveau-riche*) ..... I had once found the skeleton of a cat in the creek behind our home and had brought it inside the house to show to my mother and to my brother. My mother was horrified and had me get rid of it immediately – after all it certainly wasn't sanitary – who knows what kind of diseases we could have caught from it! Nonetheless, I definitely felt that I had been shamed and humiliated for what could be considered to be genuine scientific curiosity. Remnants of human bodies are often found by the water – one can see this in the news these days. What is the origin of this lack of tolerance that drives one to kill? It's unfathomable ....."

"Still ..... all of this environmentally degraded natural beauty was enough to take my mind off the silence of a family that spent too much time reading books. Every time we went to visit my aunt Martyra – it was usually for Easter – I would watch the 1955 version of the musical Oklahoma on the television in my aunt's den. I called it Oklahomo and in doing so – I paid homage to all of the play fags and drama queens of my high school who fancied themselves to be triple threats. They all thought that I was a bitch ….." [This was during the Post-Stonewall Pre-AIDS era when homosexual outlaws still cruised red light districts and could probably not even imagine the eventual advent of gay marriage, rainbow flags and all of the other politically-correct features of being absorbed into the majority breeder culture …..].

ALISON RANTS IN PURGATORY

Meanwhile back in Paradise ….. Alison Sh*tbox was still venting ….. "WATCH YOUR BACK, BOBBY CHUSHINGURA! ON THE BLUE GREEN PLANET – I WAS ALWAYS PLAYING THE VICTIM. FEELING SORRY FOR MYSELF AND SUCKING MY THUMB IN THE CORNER WITH A DUNCE CAP ON. AND LOOK WHERE IT GOT ME? I NEGATED MYSELF AND THEN YOU NEGATED ME! NATURE ABHORS A VACCUM

AND YOU CAME ALONG TO FILL UP MY EMPTINESS! YOU REMEMBER HOW YOU CALLED ME A SILICON-BASED LIFE FORM? YOU STOLE THAT SILICON-BASED LIFE FORM IDEA FROM THE ORIGINAL 1966-1969 STAR TREK SERIES, MR. CHUSHINGURA! YOU NEVER HAD AN ORIGINAL IDEA OF YOUR OWN IN YOUR SHORT BRUTISH LIFE! WELL YOU KNOW WHAT? YOU'RE A SHIT-BASED LIFE FORM, BOBBY C.! YOU'RE COMMON LIKE SHIT! I HOPE YOU REMAIN BOILING IN HOT STEAMING EXCREMENT UNTIL THAT TIME WHEN TWO PARALLEL LINES EVENTUALLY MEET! YOU'LL BE BOILING IN HOT BUBBLING, SIMMERING MUD CRAP UNTIL THE TWELFTH OF NEVER! AND THAT'S A LONG LONG TIME! JUST LIKE DONNY OSMOND SAID!

I'M SO GLAD THOSE DAYS OF INSECURITY AND VULNERABILITY ARE OVER! I EXIST ON A METAPHYSICAL PLANE NOW! I'M AT PEACE WITH MYSELF! THAT BEING SAID – GO FUCK YOURSELF, BOBBY! I'M PROTECTED BY THE GOLDEN-YELLOW FORCEFIELD OF RENAISSANCE ANGELS AND CHERUBS! CAN'T TOUCH THIS, BOBBY BEE-AATCH! OH THE HYPOCRISY OF ALL THOSE SEXUAL PREDATORS WHO ACTED AS IF THEY WERE SAINTS WITH HALOS! IT'S NOT MY FAULT THAT AT AGE 15 – I LOOKED LIKE I WAS GOING ON 35!

VOLODYA GUFO
Y LA FAMILIA

Volodya Gufo y La Familia

Pomposya Gufo brought forth Volodya, a protozoan wood-demon from the darkness of pre-creation, having no idea that the birth of her son would cause her such pain. He flew out of her womb like a carnivorous harpy, leaving her suffering, regretful and sore. Pomposya whispered curses to herself after his birth. She dared not say them aloud. She wanted to give Volodya a good start in life. But Pomposya's repressed hostility would ulcerate over the years and eventually she would make her son pay. She would hound him with unsolicited advice as he approached manhood. She would cause him to retreat into a fantasy world, thereby exacerbating his addictions. Years later, after his decision to dedicate himself to

Jah-Hee-Zeus had changed Volodya's heart, he called up Pomposya to tell her of his conversion (he called her "Mama"). "Mama, although formerly I was tempted by the presence of an aimless, purposeless decadence – I now trust in my goodness. Can't you see how it shines from the sockets of my eyes like a phosphorescent revelation? Know that I have been called upon by the forces of Evilangelism to clamor for war toys and wanton destruction. I will continue that age-old tradition of escalating armed conflict in Jah-Hee-Zeus' name". And with that – he grinned with the glimmering eyes of an ancient Teutonic troll.

Pomposya had become aware of her son's disturbing gifts on the eve of his 18th birthday. On that night, sitting on the darkened porch of their Crawlspace, Texas ranch ….. *the moonlight cast sinister shadows across their faces as they communicated telepathically during a staring contest ….. a family tradition used to augment the powers of manipulation necessary to conduct ethically-challenged business transactions. The amoral energy of untruth flew between them ….. nullifying any notion of moral superiority that took so much energy for each of them to* maintain. Heat lighting struck in the distance. This was a sign that Volodya's prayers to the Hawk-Headed Goddess had been answered. Volodya licked his lips, flickered his tongue suggestively and felt deliciously dirty at the thought of defying Evilangelism. [Evilangelism would never subdue his taste for German Shit Porn – Volodya was not a saint!] He surveyed the stormy horizon beyond the Crawlspace ranch. He looked up at the ominously violet-gray-black skies and extended his arms in triumph. Two bolts of lightning struck the fingertips of his upraised hands. In that instant ….. his visage became dwarfen-eared and pointy chinned ….. his eyeballs metamorphosed into mercury-metallic marbles ….. he then exhorted his future supporters in the manner of a delusional fascist ….. "Let us pray, ye Appalatchian snake handlers that done stood by me steadfastly in these troubled times". Then the revival meetin revved up full steam ….. "OH MISS TRANSSEXUAL MESOPOTAMIA OF 2900 B.C.! I WANT TO SCARE THE LIVIN DAYLIGHTS OUTTA THIS HERE COUNTRY AS MY PANTS FALL DOWN ROUN MY ANKLES AND I SWEEP JUDEO-CHRISTIANITY UNDER THE RUG. I WILL NOW ADMIT THAT I WANT THEM THAR

THREE HUNDRED PLUS MILLION SHAKIN IN THEY BOOTS! THERE AIN'T NOTHIN SO GOOD AS TERROR AND THERE JES AIN'T ENOUGH TO GO ROUND! I CARE SO MUCH BOUT MY FAITHFUL AND UNFAITHFUL ADHERENTS ALIKE THAT I WANTS TO RAISE THEY BLOOD PRESSURE, MAKE THEM SEEK PROFESSIONAL HELP AND THEN HAVE THEM EVENTUALLY FALL BACK INTO THE COMFORT ZONE OF THEY SELF-DESTRUCTIVE BEHAVIOR. THEM AIN'T BEIN STRONG ENOUGH TO MAKE IT WITHOUT ME! THUSN I WILL HAVE THEM WAYWARD GOLDEN-CALF WORSHIPPERS IN THE PALM OF MY HAND!" ..... Soon thereafter, Volodya fulfilled his dream of becoming powerful by being elected President of Amurycka Profunda and presiding over its citizens while residing in Vashink-Tone, District of Amoebia, Amurycka Profunda.

BOMBASTIKA GUFO

On the President's second day in office, his daughter Bombastika was rushed to the hospital, the victim of a drug and alcohol-fueled altercation (involving margaritas and methamphetamines) that she had initiated. She was breathing with the aid of a ventilator, blue-faced with a bandaged head and red-purple eyes so swollen that she could barely see. "¿HIJA QUE PASO? DEMASIADAS BEBIDAS ALCOHOLICAS?" her mother Natasha Gufo inquired compassionately, as she rode with her daughter in the ambulance. Natasha stayed by her daughter's bedside that night, watching the All-Jazz-Era broadcast on television. She was dutiful to her husband and tried her best to keep him well informed during family emergencies such as these. As Natasha watched the All-Jazz-Era broadcast, she couldn't help but notice that those Middle Eastern women were so stylish. They had such a way with their veils and their henna. And yet, she felt sorry that they were not able to enjoy the freedom that was the right of all repressed Amurycka Profundan Evilangelist women.

Because he thought it would be better for Bombastika to recover away from the prying eyes of the media in the District of Amoebia – Volodya Gufo used this domestic crisis as yet another excuse to resume the family hiatus in Crawlspace, Texas. It was sure great to kick back and forget that he was the leader of a nation of more than three hundred million people!

HIDEOUS EXUBERANCE

..... Volodya wound up the Victrola in the rustic guesthouse to savor *Vixens and Vipers*, one of his favorite Appalatchin love songs. He was also enchanted by the lush harmonies of *Did You Got Bit?* ..... as well as the melancholy miasma of *Snakes Killed My Mama (And I Will Always Seek Vengeance on Reptiles!)* ..... There was a shotgun propped up against a dirty corner of the cabin porch, next to a pair of underwear covered with bright yellow urine stains, discarded during the heat of the moment of a shameful extramarital tryst; a rusty tractor and a lawnmower in the overgrown *Bonnie and Clyde-esque* backyard; a Grim Reaper Scarecrow propped up on a rope-tire swing (why Boo Radley himself would have passed up this place!). Despite his preference for low-maintenance surroundings such as these – Volodya still considered himself to be an aristocrat who needed solitude to help him to procrastinate – thus avoiding creative decision-making.

Later that evening, Volodya *y su familia* physio-animated to Stonehenge to commune with Druidyck spirits worshipped by Wykkans. At this spiritualist convergence, Bombastika tried once again to get her father's attention ..... "It's called the *smashing of the forms, papi* ..... I learned about this concept in my European art history class at Southern Evilangelist University ..... By the way – is it true that an immense subterranean super-collider forms a transcontinental underground *Asses of Evil* where top-secret personnel can gain access to any one of 7 portals ..... located in Wacko, Texas; Downwardly-Mobile, Alabama; Botoxi, Mississippi; Stonehenge, Britain; Anti-Fag-Dad, Iraq; Terror-Ran, Iran; and Pyong-Yin-Yang, North Korea? It thrills me so that the Redneck Riviera may now actually have geopolitical significance! May I be admitted into the secret society of the *Asses of Evil*? Every night, I say a prayer to Barbyzonya Solar-Wind, Goddess of Hyperventilation and Empress of Neglected Southern Gothic Traumas ..... asking for her protection ....."

Volodya responded ..... "Now don't go actin all high and mighty like that thar Chiseler McClintock. I raised you to be plain-spoken and I'll whip yer hide if you start usin them big words that I ain't never understood! And if that don't work – I'll commit arson sanctioned by the highest courts in the land and burn all of yer high-fallutin books fer Christmas! And if any of them thar suicidal Isolamik extremists get wind of the location of one of them thar portals to the Asses of Evil – you will be offered to they ambassador as a sacrifice!"

Bombastika was too much of a spoiled brat to comprehend her father's severity. "Oh *papi* ..... durin my college years, how I loved drivin blindfolded down them foggy byways in the hill country with my half-Portuguese, half Ay-Rab friend Djellaba Caipirinha. Usns had cocktail-filled thermoses behind the wheel of the SUV – with the high beams on. Djellaba read in a Hollywood biography that Montgomery Clift had enjoyed pulverized sedatives mixed in with vodka and grapefruit ..... you know that I love to party and so usns wanted to try it. Usns was young and resilient enough to handle it. Don't you worry, papi ..... them sedatives was legal ..... usns warn't so foolish as to go roun inhalin no Mary-J-Wanna! (I think that them says that "Maria-Juana" in Spanish). Usns had no fear uh crashin. Our faith kept usns strong ..... so usns knowed that usns would be forgiven by our favorite deity ..... *He Who Would Not Be Loved.* If by some rare chance usns was to have been obliterated ….. usns knowed that our souls would proceed directly to the Oral Roberts University Campus Watchtower Paradise Afterlife ….."

THE KOMODO BEAST

Meanwhile ….. back at the Crawlspace Public Library (Bombastika not needing any supervision for the time being) ….. Natasha Gufo was able to get back to work. It appeared to her co-workers that she loved her career. But on this one particular day, she sat there as still as a sentinel ….. practically catatonic with her hands folded at the front desk of the linoleum-floored, tastefully wood-paneled library interior. The place was cloaked in a Bergman-esque silence ….. the weather had become unseasonably cold ….. grayish Swedish clouds hovered outside ….. the result of climatic extremes created by global warming (any publicity warning of the dangers of that phenomenon was used as toilet paper in the Gufo household). Natasha stared straight ahead, with the slightest hint of a cruel smile on her lips. Hidden under a copy of *The Ekonomyst* in the top right-hand drawer of her desk was some German Shit Porn, an enema kit, a jar of Metamucil and a copy of a booklet from her Pal-Anon group entitled *I Get Shivers From My Secret Shame*. Another selection of pornographic DVDs was at her fingertips in the lower right-hand drawer, hidden underneath a few syrupy chick flicks such as *Mistyckal Pizza-Fäce*, *Shitting in Seattle*, *Steel Fag-Hole-Yas* and *Unclean Girls*.

Natasha was approached by a male student at Crawlspace High, a tormented outcast ….. "Excuse me ma'am ….. this here book on Norse mythology is overdue and ….. well I can't afford to pay the late fees ….. daddy's outta work right now, the trailer ceilin done buckled from all the rain, my allowance's been cut ….. plus daddy's been spendin a right lotta time cuddlin up with my step-mama ….. the woman that made my real mama disappear ….. so you see I ain't got much in the way of personal space ma'am ….. specially since Daddy and I have an unspoken agreement whereby he runs his fingers over my bare buttocks with a look on his face that lies somewhere between friendliness and insanity ….. thus the library provides a haven for me from those domestic disturbances and violations of my personal space ..... I'd be more than happy to pay when I'm able ..... ma'am if you don't mind my sayin so ..... you have the most ravishin *Devil's Rain* black eyes that I ever done seen ...."

Natasha stared at the boy curiously, smilin mysteriously, eyes uh twinklin. "Well if you jes don't seem like a fine young man ..... Course I understand that these are troubled economic times and that you're a confused and terrified child ..... Don't let it trouble yer mind, sweet pea ....." Then ..... in a supremely calculated effort to connect, she quoted Demoncrat Billy Bob McClintock in a Grinch-like manner ..... "Don't think for a second that I don't feel yer pain ....."

..... Natasha's appearance started to change, eyes uh widenin, skin uh darkenin, breathin acceleratin. She metamorphosed herself into a komodo dragon with surprisingly human features ..... she transformed into a scaly reptilian creature with a cold-blooded, carnivorous face ..... that ripped through the front of her Laura Aszczlee floral print dress when it first appeared. The boy froze in terror. He stumbled backwards into a nearby shelf and fell

..... the shelves behind him collapsing like dominoes ..... previously silent readers trapped between those falling shelves. Panic ensued and everyone started screaming, scrambling and crushing one another frantically ..... those who were able to were climbing over one another trying to escape. Before the boy could recover, Natasha Gufo, who will be referred to hereafter as *The Komodo Beast*, was on top of him. She clamped her sharp teeth onto his neck. He convulsed for 15 seconds before expiring. Then the Komodo Beast decapitated him with her powerful jaws. As fountains of blood cascaded over award-winning children's books ..... the Komodo Beast exited the library through a back entrance ..... metamorphosing back into Natasha as the local authorities swarmed the library. She got into her car – unnoticed – and drove back to the ranch as if nothing had happened .....

NATASHA GUFO BACK IN HUMAN FORM

Natasha longed for a life independent of her husband. No more vacant smiles for the camera during

$5,000-per-plate dinners. She drifted into a daydream ….. "My desert isle will not be deserted. It will be filled with decadence, *joie de vivre*, beautiful bodies, empty inner lives and sexual sociopaths greedily preyin upon the vulnerable. And when I tire of all that ….. I might jes fancy a rocky outcroppin on Easter Island ….. surrounded by marine iguanas ….. with a schoolhouse fer book learnin them three R's and a small purty New England-style chapel complete with hymns sung by Welsh coal miners." She liked to tease her husband, who was driving her up the wall with sexual frustration, infidelity being out of the question (although she herself often fantasized about Billy-Bob McClintock) ….. "C'mon now, Volodyalito ….. you can pick fights all over the world, but you can't give me none of y'alls old-school Kennefunkport-style lovin? Art thou haunted perchance by the spectre of Mamacita Gufo? The All-Powerful Pomposya Gufo? Afraid that I'll turn into that castratin bitch and will start gnashin the teeth of my vagina dentata and bite off yer wiener? Volodyalito ….. sweet sexy soul music's playin in my mind and I'm makin Spanish Rice ….. it's an Afro-Dee-Zee-Ack." ….. Volodya shot back his reply – "If I told you once – I told you a thousand times wuhmyn – don't be usin that word Afrika or none of its derivatives in my presence – thereby defilin the ideological purity of our Evilangelistical home!"

HOT PEPPER BLUE

One fine morning, Natasha and Volodya's estranged daughter Hot Pepper Blue showed up unannounced at the main house of the Crawlspace ranch. Bombastika didn't even know that she had a sister. As Hot Pepper Blue arrived, Bombastika espied her long-lost sibling from the window of her upstairs bedroom. The tarty appearance of her bad-girl sister gave Bombastika goose bumps. When Natasha answered the front door – Hot Pepper Blue addressed her mother forthrightly ….. "I come to see if you'd finally accept me, Mama. It took a lot of hard work – but I am now proud to say – That I am the International Queen of Barnyard Porn". Upon hearing this, Natasha saw red ….. and once again, began to transform herself into The Komodo Beast. Just like her husband, the use of diplomacy as a means of bridge-building had failed long ago. Wisps of smoke started to trail from her nose and mouth ..... her feral amber feline-gator eyes expanding with predatory interest ..... "I will now channel the wrath of the Hawk-Headed Goddess!" the Komodo Beast proclaimed. Hot Pepper Blue backed away in horror, through the open front door, falling back onto a mattress surrounded by a camera crew awaiting her in the front yard. The Komodo Beast suddenly became docile ..... or so it appeared ..... and headed upstairs to prepare for a reading of *Wäyre the Wylde Thyngs Arghhhh* later that day at the Crawlspace Public Library. But this was merely a ruse ..... her vendetta was just beginning. Several minutes later, The Komodo Beast heard unsettling noises in the front yard and looked out of her upstairs bedroom window to see Hot Pepper Blue participating in the creation of an interracial porn film. Hot Pepper Blue was crying out for mama while her fellow porn actors had their way with her various orifices. "These are my brothers from Afrika, Mama! That's where we all come from. And there's no reason why I can't get it on with them guilt-free. I have transcended my sexual shame! And you can too, Mama!"

HIDEOUS EXUBERANCE

The Komodo Beast was horrified by what she saw. Barebacking, cunnilingus, fellatio and double penetration right before her very eyes! The Komodo Beast hovered near her bedroom window ..... gripping the curtains with her claws as she addressed the pleasure-seekers below her harshly ..... keeping out of sight all the while ..... "Blasphemers ..... in the name of Evilangelism ..... put on yer preservatives right now! I can only pray that a sweet gentle rain of penicillin, industrial-strength mouthwash and morning-after pills will wash away the bitter aftertaste of this most vile impurity ..... this impunity! ..... The spectacle of writhing uninhibited flesh was more than The Komodo Beast could bear. She stuck her dragonhead out of the window and spewed forth a white-hot stream of target vomit fire from her maw ..... instantaneously transforming the film's cast and crew into charred embers. Seeing what she had accomplished ..... the Komodo Beast raised her claws to the sky and proclaimed ..... "Lord Szczmawg be praised ..... the Moral Universe don't abide harlots, courtesans nor strumpets – and I jes be talkin bout the mens!" she giggled to herself ..... But then The Komodo Beast had second thoughts and started to blubber over the fatal consequences of her impulsive actions. The reality of what she had done set in and a minute later ..... The Komodo Beast blacked out. Her evil deeds would not go unnoticed on the pre-Judeo-Christian-Druidyck-Wykkan-anima-spirit-Geist-plane .....

BLOORN, BLOORP AND BLOORA

The Komodo Beast found herself trapped and unable to move in the bottom of a pit that was used to capture wild animals. Her plight was being overseen by The Three Emissaries of Valhaha – Bloorn, Bloorp, and Bloora. They were two brutish male Vikings and one pale woolven-fanged Icelandick demi-goddess – three blonde, vampirick death metallites – all of them smartly dressed in cloaks of black and bedecked in primitive Nordick-Celtick silver ..... How had The Komodo Beast arrived there? She pressed her hands to her cold cheeks and realized that she was not dreaming. She started to shake with the fear of death ..... was this the end? The Three Emissaries circled around the edge of the pit. Bloorn, Bloorp, and Bloora chanted melodies from Runick texts in Old Norse as a blackened church smoldered in the background – these were their pagan rituals. They kept a careful eye on the Komodo Beast as they taunted her in a spirit of faux innocence ….. "Who will save thee now, Lady Mini-Nuke?" "Now thou shalt fall into the clutches of the Frog Prince!" "This Aristocratick Amphibian will most assuredly amuse thee." "Twould it not have been simpler to embrace those spirits whose essential nature thou denied?" And finally ….. "Her no am sexy dragon – Her make bitter fire!"

Bloorn, Bloorp and Bloora continued to mock the Komodo Beast as they drank their fill of mead that night to celebrate. The Komodo Beast was given a hefty dosage of an ancient organic sedative that made her as docile as a kitten. The next morning, The Three Emissaries packed up their belongings and disappeared into the fog of the nearby hill country. The Komodo Beast accompanied them. They walked her on a leash to their world ….. where she became their slave …..

GOTHRA SCHVULKOPF AND THE DAILY GRIND

Gothra Schvulkopf and the Daily Grind

Gothra Schvulkopf was fed up. She pulled down her khakis, mooned the camera and spun her bare ass around on a Mistyckal Pizza at 186,000 miles per second. Stainless steel appliances flew out of her mouth and asshole as her hands modestly covered her steamy groin à la Sandro Botticelli. "After I take off my fig leaf – I use it in soups and leftovers! Make the school children cover their eyes as I get it on with an Amsterdam prostitute in her cubicle! Mama's been workin hard and she wants a reward!" she wailed ..... Gothra was cooking on all four burners. Sugar caramelizing in a saucepan on the stove; *baba au rhum* in the oven; organic coffee and champagne enemas alternately pumping out her shit stream between on-camera takes. Gothra was a whirling dervish ….. "Yesterday I covered the entire interior surface of a Chelsea gallery with spinach lasagna and then coated it with polyurethane to create my first multi-media, multi-sensory *découpage* installation. It's a smorgasbord for the senses featuring a sound-collage of celebrity ring tones blaring in echo chambers, recordings of me barking out orders to my frightened assistants, an authentic soundtrack from the construction of a post 9-11 East Village skyscraper and a kitsch repackaging of circa 1965 Haight Ashbury light shows on film. To top it off ….. a French maid in the style of Toulouse Lautrec serves hors-d'oeuvres with a flashlight in the pitch-black main room of the exhibition space ….. three corners of which are in utter darkness. In the fourth corner, like the pink candle of an Advent wreath and lit from above, a man covered entirely in rubber fetish gear crouches silently on all fours ….. waiting for his torturer ….. only his mouth is visible ….. "

Before each on-camera appearance, Gothra chanted the mantras that had gotten her to the top and that were keeping her there ….. me *not sexy hot, me not sexy hot, me not sexy hot ..... love make me not work, love make me not work, love make me not work ..... makey more time, makey more time, makey more time.* After saying each affirmation three times – she then jingled the keys to any of her numerous safe deposit boxes to complete the ritual, segueing smoothly to the on-camera copy: ..... "My hair is ash-sand blonde, my skin geisha-white, my eyes as black as the deepest subterranean caves of Morewhore. One can espy an Amazonian jungle creeping along the edge of my bikini line. Little children burn doggie poo in paper bags on my doorstep on Halloween and run away cackling in the harvest moon dry brown leaf rustling night ..... That's all for now folks! Got to crank out some mo smelly black bean malaria swamp horsefly mud pies!" At the end of her presentation, a fed-up union stagehand whispers to a co-worker ..... *this bitch is goin to give me cancer!* In the meantime ..... in a parallel universe .... on the rocky shores of an underground lake beneath the cavernous rafters of Gothra's soul ..... the dormant orgasmic female within her was lush, vulnerable and easily satisfied.

HIDEOUS EXUBERANCE

Gothra returned to the set after a short catnap, raring to go. "And now – my recipe for Aztec Middl Earf Hampton prune compote. I recommend being in shape to prepare this recipe ..... but you'll need more than just aerobics. My to-do list would wind an Olympic sprinter. First and foremost ..... remember how important it is to cleanse. Take laxatives and amphetamines and shit out your insides. I tried that lemon cayenne pepper honey diet ..... but oh Maya Hiyuh Powuh! The heartburn! ..... Okay here we go – Place your unwashed hands into a bowl of elephant feces (yes it's an acquired taste). Set the bowl of elephant shit aside to cool for one half-hour. Then stand up and shovel horse manure into a vat of dark syrupy prunes. Macerate the prunes into a brown purple mélange while thinking of Tahitian sunsets, pristine arctic environments, and the tropical soil of a post-napalm-era Vietnamese jungle. Chug down a Metamucil fruit shake and then collapse into a vat of steamed Turkish apricots. Place your bare buttocks into an open window on the top floor of the Empire State Building and blow out whatever's left inside. Then place the prunes, apricots and elephant feces into a mixing bowl, adding your pee pee gradually, until the proper consistency has been achieved. Freeze the resulting compote overnight in Tupperware bowls and serve at absolute zero with a big scoop of petrified Pompeian Tofutti-based-non-dairy frozen topping .....

Finally ..... witness an exhibition of the weapons of mass destruction concealed in the crootches of a roomful of hot sexy studs. Sexual shame is not an option here, ladies. I'm living a different life when the cameras are turned off ..... and I know that you are too! Tear off your bras, throw them into a bonfire and go streaking like it was 1973! When I want to relax – I bury myself up to my neck in hot sulfurous brown red ochre mustard clay. Either that – or I submerge myself in worm-filled purple gray brownie mix that feels so fantastically icky! *¡Tenemos que usar todos los colores!*" Spanish has become so popular in the ever-evolving melting pot that is Amurycka Profunda! *¡Me gusta cocinar! ¡Soy la cocinera!* At the end of your mud bath ..... cool down in one of three ways: (1) revel in the shame – go out and self-destruct with the addiction of your choice; (2) find a quiet space in a Japanese teahouse for prayer or meditation. Make contact with the God of your choosing ..... Great Spirit, Cosmic Creator, The Source, The Universe, Goddess; or (3) Moan, wail, howl, scream, beg, repent and make demands of the voices in your head in that conference room where you usually masturbate."

Gothra had recently guest-starred as "The Exhibitionist" on a new Russian reality TV show entitled *Mooskaya Djzhaynszczeena*. Barefoot and topless, sporting only a pearl necklace, an old pair of beige khakis that she used for gardening at Beef Jerky Mill [her headquarters in Mistykk, Kinetykk-Koont] and a preppy blue and green whale belt – she let her hair down and shook her maracas, continuing with her on-camera copy ..... "My gentle onscreen purring is a complete lie, ladies and gentlemen. And here's the evidence ..... check out this song that I wrote! Tis all about carob, unsweetened baker's chocolate and filthy gas station bathrooms (the kind favored by fugitive serial killers in Salinas, California). Don't fall for those seductive yet pock-faced Western gas station attendants. Use your credit card at the self-serve station; you can always go online later that night if you're looking for Mr. Wrong (in that regard, I prefer hook-up sites featuring narcissistic muscle queens with no less than 18 beguiling poses – they're often gifted florists as well!). Chances are those gas station attendants are psychopaths who will cut off your head and put it in their freezer ….. eradicating your chances for existential success. That's it in a nutshell – please excuse me for my momentary lack of professionalism – but I forgot the rest of this monologue. There's so much going on. I'm preoccupied with the management of my real estate holdings. 10 houses means 100 different wallpaper decisions! Mama has to do it all herself ….. she doesn't trust anyone ….. " Gothra belched violently – then hurried to her green room for a five-minute aromatherapy break. She inhaled a potent potpourri comprised of lavender, sandalwood, juniper, verbena, peppermint, dehydrated blood orange and cedar. She returned to the set a refreshed and reinvigorated organic machine …..

"….. Moving right along ….. this pastel peach porcelain bowl was given to me as a gift by a sadistic Prussian king. He sold me the most fabulous antiques from the Austro-Hungarian Empire for a steal! I like to run my fingertips along the cool base of this bowl

HIDEOUS EXUBERANCE

(I actually transcend time and space in the process). I keep this particular piece on display on a slab of black marble, lit with pin spots, in a corner of the living room of my Middl Earf Hampton villa. The marble slab is supported by the outstretched arms of a fossilized Wagnerian dwarf. Tune in tomorrow night for a master course on the creation of pungent fudge poo pie!" ..... Gothra left the set in a huff, chastising her assistant for not boiling lemon rinds to freshen the air in her dressing room. Later that evening, Gothra relieved some stress by building a tree house entirely out of foam core in the backyard of her villa.

AN ENCOUNTER WITH THE KOMODO BEAST

Gothra had good reason to snap at her overworked and underpaid assistant. She was recovering from a traumatic hazing inflicted on her by the bloodthirsty Komodo Beast (AKA *Natasha Gufo*). Gothra had been held hostage in a rusty tin shack in a desolate area of Guavantanamo Bay on a tropical island not far from the borders of southeast

Amurycka Profunda – where she had been tortured by The Komodo Beast and her assistant Prometheus Sludge [the Pink Brown Soothsayer and the Pseudo-Druidyck High Priest of Sex and Shit]. Gothra remained haughty at first – trying to extract information from her torturer. With the combined forces of Mata Hari and Julia Child, she steeled herself and gathered up her inner strength ….. *"JUST WHO THE HELL ARE YOU, PROMETHEUS SLUDGE?!?!"* she demanded. But she was unable to maintain her nonchalant attitude when deep bloody slashes created canyons across her ass cheeks after a caning. The day after that abuse, Gothra was taken outside by her captors at dusk – "to prevent dementia" she was told. The Komodo Beast, eyes shining bronze mercury, planted one scaly leg-limb up on a tree stump and lit up a big fat cigar like she was Ma Joad from *The Grapes of Wrath*. The Komodo Beast proceeded to gesticulate against the backdrop of a vibrant Okie sunset as Prometheus Sludge stared at Gothra with a look of sullen insanity. The Komodo Beast spoke to Gothra in a menacing tone ….. "Here's yer answer bout Prometheus Sludge, missy! Sludge ain't no campfire ghost from yer romanticized childhood! Sludge is a soulless killin machine born in the hot volcanic mud of Morewhore. Him got wide-open snow-white eyes, a mud-encrusted lizardy body and a male Medusa smile that beckons yet repulses ….. I once reveled in witnessin the sheer grace of his killin prowess while reclinin on the bank of the Mississippi River near Vicksburg under the cool shade of a weepin willow with a banjo on my knee and a powdered-wig 18th century-lookin faggot playin harpsichord nearby ….. Once in the clutches of Sludge, chances fer survival are slim. Sludge does his best work in southern Louisiana where him drags his victims down into a bubblin gator-filled bayou ….. asphyxiatin them while whisperin sweet nothins in they ears. Them deceased victims are then converted into meaty praline candies and sold on Bourbon Street to fat-ass drunken revelers drinkin beer outta plastic cups."

"I AIN'T UH SKEERED UH NO PROMETHEUS SLUDGE!" Gothra shouted back, her fists shaking with rage. "You don't know who you're dealing with. I was hired by Fairy-Man to uproot trees with my bare hands. To prepare his war-machine of Morewhorian Blorks for a face-off with Gondolphus Clownhouse, a great WYSIWYG wizard known to dance the night away beating on his tambourine with flamboyantly effeminate abandon. If only them Enyuh Trees hadn't come along and stopped the evil work we was doin!"….. Gothra regained her composure and slipped back into her seductive cooking-show accent ….. "Little did Fairy-Man know that I was a double agent for Snore-On [the Dark Prince of Morewhore] when I was doing research for *Dying Magazine*. We made such beautiful music together cramming tasteful publicity down the public's throats. Back during the time when I was a stockbroker – I had once ridden on the back of the Dollblog. I was testing my tenacity – I'm always up for a challenge! ….. We circled around the Bottomless Pit of Middl Earf Hampton – I wouldn't be where I am right now if I wasn't accustomed to taking these kinds of risks. I tamed this behemoth with the prospect of myriad macaroni and cheese casseroles prepared in *Le Crever* porcelain cookware [No toxic Gaymart Tephlaan for me]! For that, Gondolphus Clownhouse will always be grateful. The Dollblog – being the essence of smothering-abandoning maternal femininity – was too much for poossy-hating Clownhouse. It was the take-charge castrating bitch in me that helped me to deflate the Dollblog's sails. And when the opportunity came along to work for Fairy-Man, I had to grab it. He was the gatekeeper of a demographic that I alone could cultivate. Maya Hiyuh Powuh knows that I'd be nowhere if I had integrity! And Fairy Man pays way better than Gaymart – that's for sure!"

GOTHRA'S THEATRICAL DEBUT

Gothra, in her ever-expanding campaign for greater fame, had landed the role of anti-heroine Misty "La Misère" McGonagall in a production of *Howl: A Musical Exorcism* (adapted from the poem by Aloe-Vera Ginseng). Gothra thought that the singing and dancing would give her some relief from her pressure-cooker, domestic diva lifestyle. Although not blessed with natural talent as a performer, she had nonetheless been expecting a standing ovation after her supposed-to-be-show-stopping number – *Go Find a Friend and Step on Their Dream*. But when the stares and stony silence of the audience made her realize that these spectators didn't love her as an entertainer ..... memories of her father barking at her over the intercom he'd installed in her bedroom as a teenager filled her with rage. This audience had found out that she wasn't good enough ..... and that was unacceptable to Gothra ..... She left the theatre fuming and took a cab downtown to the Stonewall Bar, a place where she felt better than everybody else ..... "Maybe one of these faggy fags will want to work for me and in the process I can deprive him of his paycheck!" she calculated, after undertipping the cab driver as was her custom.

Assisted by her faithful Pumpkin Trolls, who she could summon in an instant via the Harridan Square Wormhole (this wormhole functioned as a portal to Gothra's various estates; she also made use of it for time travel) – she quelled her bristling anger by randomly picking a shifty hoostler out of the crowd and smacking him upside the head with a shovel [Gothra and her Pumpkin Trolls always kept shovels handy for impromptu gardening]. She lifted him over her head, grabbed onto his wrists, spun him around like a lasso, then slammed him onto his back on the floor of the bar. She kicked him in the chin, ribs, and crootch (she was taking care of Frances Farmer's unfinished business!). She tied a rope around his ankles, dragged him outside to the northeast corner of 7th Avenue and Krissuhfuh Street, spun him around over her head at an incalculable velocity and then tossed him into traffic, where he was immediately squashed by a cab, bones cracking, horrified onlookers aghast. She went back into the bar, shooting molten lava from her eyes, literally petrifying everyone in the place, including the husband and wife summer stock team by the piano who were singing *You'll Never Walk Alone*.

Gothra was handed a megaphone by her Pumpkin Trolls after this *coup de grâce* to address the patrons of the bar ….. "Hey everybody! Forget this guy! I'll make a savory quiche from his brains – that my Pumpkin Trolls will shovel up from the scene of the accident! My resources are never wasted! ….. Listen up ladies! Here's yet another plan that I devised during a recent bout of insomnia. It concerns the creation of a 50-tiered devil's food cake with red, white and blue vanilla butter-cream frosting. It'll be the size of a football field. As usual, you can thank me for getting your sedentary asses in gear. Cement mixers will provide the frosting. We'll be spackling sticky sweetness all through the night with a diverse variety of human-sized putty knives – stainless steel, plastic and wood – all of them produced by my Gaymart design team. Heelmoot Nu-Tone's protégé [Phygg Nu-Tone] and I will be multi-tasking and cross promoting by photographing the event for a coffee table book we're working on together. So defy me if you can with your shields of Tupperware, your Melmak helmets and your pineapple-porcupine chastity belts ….. you debased and degraded obese bitches!"

Gothra grabbed onto a fragrant bag of potpourri that she had concealed in the left-hand pocket of her cocoa brown suede-leather jacket. She inhaled deeply, put the bag back into her pocket and continued with her tirade ….. "Don't be intimidated by the tension and danger that is present in Heelmoot Nu-Tone's meisterwerk *Snorefleisch*. Just remember this ….. the Euripidean decadence of the late-phase Western world has acted as a crucible for a preponderance of homosexual *ennui* ….. a microcosm of that reality being represented by the clientele of this bar. Personally, Heelmoot Nu-Tone disgusts me! He's so damn sexually liberated! But oh how I envy him! In my mind, I want to fuck everything that moves. But in reality, I'm so prissy! A downright prude! Voilà ..... in our book, Phygg Nu-Tone and I will combine the following images ..... Harlequin Romance covers, muscular bisexual sadists, nubile nymphs from the *Ancien Regime*, unabashedly proud Sin-Torrids, geeky computer nerds engaging in webcam cybersex, couch-potato trailer-trash inhaling Cheez-Doodles in the pale blue TV light and Evilangelists looking at pornography ..... Remember that I am politically neutral. I will always support the Radical Right as long as they buy my products. Finally ..... I am designing state-of-the-art kitchenware that will resist nuclear devastation!" ..... After she had finished her pronouncement, Gothra politely paid for her Curaçao margarita, left the bar and traveled by physio-animation via the Harridan Square Wormhole to a parking lot nearby her Middl Earf Hampton villa in Eastern Long Guile-Land. Twenty minutes later, she pulled into the driveway of the villa, turned off the lights and the engine and fell asleep

GOTHRA SCHVULKOPF AND THE DAILY GRIND

at the wheel. She woke up with the sunrise feeling refreshed.

Gothra needed a break – she was worn out. So she escaped to the Not-So-Great Hall of Snore-On, where she read jaw-dropping poetry with compelling conviction to an open mike full of astonished, gaping Blorks (Gothra never forgot her failures – after the humiliating debacle that was *Howl: A Musical Exorcism* – she was going to grab an audience by the balls if it killed her). Gothra had recently been given a merry-go-round, a gift from Snore-On that she had installed on the grounds of her Middl Earf Hampton villa. Snore-On had praised her condescendingly during their last meeting ….. "I learned so much about pure evil from you, dear. And I wanted so very much to return the favor. This will be your Neverland ….. now get on that merry-go-round and go back to the imaginary childhood you never had! The one where all the kids in your neighborhood liked you because they had no idea that you'd grow up to be a ball-breaking home economist who'd be too busy to play fair." Gothra, inspired by Snore-On's sycophantic praises, stripped off all of her clothes and proceeded to use the merry-go-round to act out the fantasies of her solitary *Snorefleisch* eroticism. At this point, she was drunk and practically howling at the moon ….. "TURN ON THE FLOODLIGHTS, SNORE-ON! I WANT EVERYONE TO SEE ME IN MY BIRTHDAY SUIT!" she barked at her frienemy ….. As she held on tightly to the pony poles she moaned, shivered and pleasured herself with the cold, shiny, artificial brilliance of the lacquered horses ….. slobbering over their inanimate mouths.

The next day on the set, Gothra filmed a TV special in the backyard of Beef Jerky Mill. A fan called in during the proceedings ….. *Hi Gothra! I'm lying on a dirty mattress in a cold attic phantasming about you! This is the headquarters for my underground talk radio show / pod-people cast! I was born on the Blue Purple Brown Algae Sewage Planet and I write for Mush, a magazine that appeals to the lowest instincts of mankind! We're based inside the frigid ash gray white cone of an extinct volcano in Kamchatka, Anti-Amurycka Profunda. By the way – I'm wild for your Peppermint Sphincter Scrub! Bye bye itchy hemorrhoidal asshole! Peppermint Sphincter Scrub is the answer to my prayers! Have a word for our subscribers, Gothra?*

THE REINVENTION OF GOTHRA

But before Gothra had a chance to respond – The Komodo Beast appeared out of nowhere. The Komodo Beast had been sent by the Three Emissaries of Valhaha – *deus ex machina*-style – to light a fire under Gothra's asexual, atrophied buttocks with a carpet of bluish flames. Gothra was then transported to a semi-arid purgatory, where she proceeded to cultivate a Mediterranean garden [and so this purgatory came to be known as *Mediterrogatory*]. The garden became her *modus operandi*, her sole obsession, her *raison d'etre*. Just at the apex of the explosion of its blooms ….. Mediterrogatory would suddenly dehydrate ….. turning brown, brittle and lifeless before bursting into flames and being reduced to a pile of cinders. No phoenix ever rose from these ashes. Gothra had to start from scratch, which always pleased her ….. her work in this limbo had led her back to the joy of the creative process again and again. She was making the best of an eternally frustrating situation.

But before all of that, as she was being whisked away – Gothra had a final word for her fans ..... "Don't waste your shit! Just make sure it's steaming hot in a Ziploc bag when you send it to my Foundation for the Improvement of Amurycka Profundan Cuisine. I need to know that you're being productive! We'll grow vegetables with it! What the public doesn't know won't hurt them! Take a Polaroid of yourself making a face while you evacuate your bowels – but don't push too hard! Don't give those hemorrhoids a chance to flower! On the other hand – remember that for just $300 per hour – I will make house calls and apply vitamin E to your respective burning sphincters. I know what I'm doing. My Peperoncino Anti-Hemorrhoid Scrub is flying off the shelves! [No need for a stop-loss order in this instance!] Call my 800 number! I'll be in the garden – 1-800-THEGRDN! However, that service will be entirely automated. If you think that you're going to get a live person on the phone – forget it! In closing – God's ugliest creatures from the darkest depths of the deepest oceans will dine on my poossy in Valhaha!" ..... In a final flourish, Gothra blew a kiss to her fans while looking directly into the camera, crying tears of blood ..... "I'll never forget you, Joisey City!" she blubbered .....

After a hard day's work in Mediterrogatory, Gothra was always exhausted. But she never forgot how to live well. Every night, she slept in a bathtub filled with Vaseline, mint-chocolate biscotti, and Asian long-horned beetles. The Pumpkin Trolls covered her with desert flowers, baobab sprouts, volcanic topsoil and peat moss while serenading her with sarcastic lullabies .....

GOTHRA SCHVULKOPF AND HER PUMPKIN TROLLS

Gothra Schvulkopf and her Pumpkin Trolls

Gothra shoved her ass into a hole of hot red Martian sand. This cold planet had its fiery core heated by the Dollblog – who had recently physio-animated from the Bottomless Pit of Middl Earf Hampton to stalk Gothra, to reclaim Mars as its territory and to officially recognize dark matter as an essential building block of the Universe. As Gothra saw it, she and her business could not thrive without the Dollblog-heated Martian biosphere – and therefore compromise was necessary. She took a meeting with the Dollblog, at which time he gave her an ultimatum ….. human sacrifices would be required as a tribute. After the profits from her latest venture started rolling in, she would travel to other planets to establish new outposts, in the process leaving her witless assistants behind to be devoured by the Dollblog. At least that was what Gothra agreed to do ….. on the record. However, she had other plans ….. It was here on Mars that Gothra had at last found a refuge from her competitors ….. "All of those Middl Earf Hampton bitches who attempted to challenge me have been vanquished. And upon hearing the news that all of the garbage produced by the Blue Green Planet is now being shipped to a black hole at the edge of the galaxy on a regular basis – I was thrilled! Recycling is the way of the future! I looked into my crystal ball and I saw opportunity here. I will exploit this hungry maw of negative energy. I will find a new way to heat this planet and to send the Dollblog packing to be crushed in a singularity. I will be the first state-of-the-art home economist to conquer the galaxy. Besides ….. this Martian biosphere supports my habit of Mediterranean and Japanese picnicking ….."

"….. The Blue Green Planet is my Mother Goddess! I feel so inspired by her! She makes me want to get foocked by a suicide bomber on top of the Fresh Kills Landfill. That's right – bring on the decadence! Although I've never been known for my slutty side – that could change! For years now, I've sacrificed my craving for sensual pleasures for the sake of success. I've always valued quality over quantity. As much as I'm partial to Baroque instrumentation and candle lit film sets à la *Barry Lyndon* ….. the *G. I. Jane* in me wants to get up and go ballistic in one of those wide-ass Hummer things. I'll go to Eye-Rack – I'll go to Kaftanistan! I'll develop *prêt-a-porter* body armor for the troops just to get me through a Tarkovskian weekend of devastating loneliness. I'll run down the dry, dusty streets with my Kalishnikov in dirty camouflage fatigues ….. heaving grenades into the homes of doomed consumers ….. who will never have the chance to experience post-Gothra-product-purchase-afterglow. I'll kick ass in Eye-Rack and Kaftanistan! This will also be a great opportunity for me to publicize my new clothing line – *War Whore*. The camouflage fatigues I'll be sporting to advertise this product will be available in aqua-powder blue, olive-tan green and red-brown cedar ….. colors reminiscent of Provence. Yet know that I am pragmatic. I'll scurry down the streets at sunset in a burka if I have to and I will make that curfew ….."

Whenever she became too introspective, Gothra had to freeze her heart and get back to work. She allowed herself only 5 minutes a day of emotional, spiritual, and philosophical reflection. Her fans were only interested in the consumer-friendly products that constituted her bottom line. If she happened to have some unexpected downtime and found her fingers wandering towards her warm nether regions, she had to remind herself that it was sexual suppression that had gotten her that Gaymart contract. If Gothra were to ever confront her inner truth ….. her empire would be ruined. Her latest success-affirming monologue went something like this ….. "My frigidity DEFINITELY helped me to become a BILLIONAIRESSE and there's NO QUESTION that it was WORTH IT. Sex without love is merely COMPULSION ….. so I haven't missed A THING. My sexuality is now SUBLIMINALLY CHANNELED into my QUEST FOR WORLD DOMINATION. I made a really STUPID COMMENT about Nielsen Mandala's 27-year prison term on Fairie Queene Dead. I compared it to my 5 month SLAP ON THE WRIST where I fooled myself into thinking that I was a HUMANITARIAN by teaching some PRISON LAIDIES arts and kräfts behind bars.

And here's another thing that I don't understand ..... I'm so down with black people ..... I'm FOONCKY, I can MOOOOVE, I'm not afraid to SHAAAKE IT. Just because I'm not getting any doesn't mean that I'm not SEXY and UNASHAMED. But recreational leisure of that nature is so very TIME-CONSUMING. So I SACRIFICED that side of myself that struts down dark alleyways as a NYMPHO-MANIACAL Vivienne Lay. Being powerful is VERY STRESSFUL but my REAL ESTATE HOLDINGS nurture me in a way MOOMIE NEVER COULD. Finally — I have the PSYCHIC SPACE I longed for in my childhood ..... If ONLY I could just LEAVE IT ALONE ..... If only I could just LET IT BE .....

Gothra retreated into a waking dream ..... *She was dressed as the Nimoy-Spock of circa 1966 Star Trek for her upcoming Halloween TV-special and was wandering around the set of Salem's Lot, thinking to herself ..... "I really must figure out a function for my ass that's related to my business. Since it's usually sexually inactive ..... I think I'll write it off as a loss. Maybe I could keep it cool with liquid nitrogen?" (Gothra's perfectionism drained her — but it was the only way she knew) ..... Then she was hiding in a* dark closet gnawing on a dog bone, salivating with piercing, phosphorescent red eyes. Any little children unfortunate enough to pass by her closet where she crouched like a werewoolf would be instantaneously devoured (years of ardent professionalism had created this volcano that was simmering and ready to explode). Then she shoved wheelbarrows full of Hassenpfeffer-Ridge Farm cookies into her mouth until she blew up to the size of Jobba the Koont. She loved fresh pepper too ..... fresh pepper was her porn. She was also crazy about dark chocolate and was constantly reminding her fans how good it was for them! She bought it wholesale whenever she was in Brussels ..... a city that disgusted her due of its lack of feng shui. In defiance of the city's ugliness and its pooper-scooper law (je ramasse!) she evacuated her colon in narrow 18th century alleyways, looking both ways to make sure that she wasn't being watched .....

..... Gothra snapped out of her daydream and for a split second considered neglecting the mountain of tasks that awaited her. Sometimes success bored her and she considered going back to her working-class roots to do some catering for Space Station Mir.

GOTHRA SCHVULKOPF AND HER PUMPKIN TROLLS

She could relate to those Russian cosmonauts on a dark Slavic level. To avoid a potential slip into apathy – Gothra repeated several affirmations that were a part of her spiritual discipline – before rolling up her sleeves and striding into a boardroom full of Gaymart executives to start pitching ideas. After that meeting, she made the following notes to herself ….. "I pitched the following idea for a billboard to the Gaymart suits. At first they hated it – but I remedied that by shoving Tupperware containers full of steak tartar down their throats – until they decided to support my campaign. The billboard will feature a picture of me naked à la Heelmoot Nu-Tone. I'll be posing doggy-style with the palms of my hands on the floor and my tax write-off ass facing an audience of rush-hour commuters on a suburban highway. Underneath this image, the following copy will appear…..

"*It's so easy to expand your fan base. First ….. clean out your colon. Death starts in the colon. Upon the completion of this simple act ….. everything else will fall into place. If you don't have the willingness, if your intention is not aligned with your integrity, even a Herculean effort won't take you where you want to* go. Creative visualization will enable you to materialize an enema bag out of thin air and to jump-start the propulsive power of your spasmodic, gyrating intestinal gavotte. Look at my hands – although they have been weathered by years of intensive gardening – these are the hands of my ancestors. The hands of women who birthed their babies out in the fields and kept on working immediately after childbirth. They didn't have Cymbalta and they were just fine! I honor that Great Chain of Being! If I can inspire even one career-hating commuter residing in the suburban wasteland of Amurycka Profunda ….. that will be a win-win …..

….. Creative visualization will bring you untold rewards ….. never mistrust it. The early stages of this campaign were conceived during insomniac nights at Beef Jerky Mill. I had become obsessed with devising new ways of shortchanging my staff and I needed a distraction ….. I recommend a cross-country trip by car! If you haven't been inspired by the big skies of Amurycka Profunda – you haven't lived! ….. I will leave you with these words of wisdom, messieurs dames ….. I am the red rose that bleeds well concealed in the heart of a pine-green-blooded Vulcan ..... I will now fly in my Chartreuse Hybrid Priapus directly onto the rings of Saturn ..... where I will open up a lemonade-urine stand. My entrepreneurial vision has no limits! This will be the fulfillment of the dream of a lifetime ..... Goodbye! Time for my miso soup break! Miso flushes radioactivity out of the system ....."

After the completion of her presentation, Gothra stepped into an empty conference room, sipped from a cup of piping hot jasmine green tea and recorded new notes to herself ..... "My next TV special will encompass the following themes ..... the travails of the Siberian shaman, the octoroons of Cajun country and controversial methods utilized in the production of ethanol. In moments of extreme crisis, I marvel at my durability. For instance ..... there was that time when I held my daughter Elysia over a hotel balcony in Dubai and shook all of the change, consisting of the 16 major currencies of the Blue Green Planet, out of her pockets. No one can tell me what to do with my daughter. After all, I created her. Like Kali–Shiva ..... I am the Creator and the Destroyer." Then Gothra closed her eyes for a moment of prayer directed towards her idols in the Great Chain of Being ….. *Fill my hemlock cup to the brim with Tyrolean purple, Svengalska Rasputinovich. Your clairvoyance may amaze ….. but my encyclopedic knowledge of Velcro and Post It Pads makes me the true existentialist* ….. Gaymart's car service drove her home to Beef Jerky Mill that night. Upon her arrival, she glanced through back issues of *Architectural Digest* and *House Beautiful*. Half an hour had been set aside to do so …..

SMOKEY BUBBLES AND BILLY TIRADE

Smokey Bubbles – an overweight, drunken, red-faced white middle manager sporting a pink button-down – was discussing Gothra with his co-worker at a karaoke party in a bar nearby Battery Park, Nueva Jork. He had worked with Gothra on Wall Street years before and was killing some time talking about her – as he was not looking forward to taking the 7 line home to Flushing that evening. How he envied the fearlessness with which she had pursued her dream! "Billy – the thing I could never figure out bout that bitch was whether she wanted a coock, a poossy or nothin." Smokey's associate, Billy Tirade, responded. "Hold that thought Smokey – I have to take a dump." Smokey came right back at him. "Hey Billy, speakin uh dumps – I hoyd dat Gothra likes to have duh guy fuckin dump in huh fuckin mouth."

Back in her ominous gray-black stone castle, the crown jewel of her Middl Earf Hampton properties, a green-faced *Wykked* Gothra laughed hysterically for a few minutes as she gazed at Smokey and Billy in her crystal ball. Then she slipped into the meditative silence of her inner monologue, inspired by her gratitude for the guidance of Kali-Shiva Creator-Destroyer ..... *Say what you will fellas. Acceptance is the answer to all of my problems today. This castrating bitch is laughing all the way to the bank. My creativity transcends moral censorship. In my latest attempt at re-invention ..... my combined vagina-colon will expand to swallow its victims like a Venus flytrap. I am the fallopial-intestinal-supercollider that functions in that twilight zone between blood and shit. I am the sprightly vampirick infant that dances around the maypole of the fetal chamber in anticipation of a Kevorkian-induced coma ......*

GOTHRA BACK IN HER ELEMENT

Back at Beef Jerky Mill, it was an enchanting spring morning in the third week of May as Gothra pressed down on a shovel with her strong wiry foot to sow her latest batch of pumpkin seeds. 4 months later on a clear frosty morning – she led her Pumpkin Trolls through the autumn fields to harvest the product. "Let's get going, ye faithful servants of my dynasty ..... just remember that I crack the whip. We have no time to waste ..... there's a mountain of spectrally-ordered monogram sweaters waiting at home that must be folded before noon". The Pumpkin Trolls smiled back brilliantly. They had perfected the art of passive-aggressive manipulation – it was the only way they could tolerate the constant stream of abuse. In their downtime, The Pumpkin Trolls dreamt of revenge and anarchy, as It was never too early for Gothra to start raging. "I want the biggest, fattest pumpkins. I am hungry for orange, hungry for the color that will make my viewers salivate as they sit on their ever-expanding asses. The inhabitants of Amurycka Profunda are getting fatter and fatter and I want all of the money that they're not spending at the gym. I hope that they'll clean out their 401Ks and clear the shelves of my sheets and towels! Pumpkin Trolls ….. after our work here is done, I'll need you to prepare PowerPoint pie charts for a midtown Manhattan breakfast meeting. It's with the Gaymart executives and it's tomorrow at 8 a.m. sharp. The subject we'll be discussing is a low fat, high carb cookie that guarantees severe obesity."

That night, Gothra had a dream (stress was wreaking havoc on her REM sleep but occasionally images from her subconscious workings broke through) ….. *A brawny butterscotch tiger cat with chartreuse eyes was sleeping peacefully on the top of a 1940s hutch next to two pumpkins, a bottle of Camus and two crystal decanters ….. one containing Johnnie Walker Black, the other Glenfiddich single malt scotch whisky* ….. Gothra awoke the next day reinvigorated. The earthy browns and oranges of her dream guided her through her agenda. Those colors would soon be present throughout the latest issue of *Dying Magazine* – that featured Gothra on the cover flying over Mars disguised as a giant bumblebee – in a takeoff of *Total Recall*. As her dream life was now calling to her with alarming frequency – Gothra got into the habit of taking catnaps. Her right and left brain were engaged in a heated shouting match and since neither side was going to give – they fought until they were exhausted – falling down to pass out in a Budweiser-stained beanbag chair in the basement of an Off-Off-Broadway black box theatre circa 1995 (one never knew where Gothra would end up on any given day) .....

..... *Gothra was transported back to a witch burning in 1692 Salem, Massachusetts via the Harridan Square Wormhole. She was dancing a jig by a bonfire with the Pumpkin Trolls nearby the edge of Lucifer's dark piney woods on the outskirts of town. But these Pumpkin Trolls looked decidedly different than those employed by Gothra. They were exotic Eurasian leprechauns from the lands of the Tatar in the Russian steppes. While dancing, they spoke a Finno-Ugric tongue and practiced shamanic rites* common among Ural-Altaic cultures. They smiled viciously and dreamt of revenge like their waking-life counterparts. Spirits summoned by the leprechauns took possession of Gothra ..... who was suddenly hurling out curses in an extinct Gaelic tongue ..... as a huge red sun rose over a bubbling lake of orange lava. Hellish cries of pain were heard in the background. Gothra sailed by on a raft, serenely oblivious, keeping a watchful eye on yet another perfect crème brûlée [how does she do it?] piping away on a cookie sheet attached to the back of the raft. With one hand, she kept three Morewhorian Blorks on a leash. With the other hand, she held out a tray of sugar cookies. But these were no ordinary sugar cookies. They had been sprinkled with a lifetime of bitterness. Gothra sighed and then cried out to the Goddess of Her Understanding, Maya Hiyuh Powuh ..... "Know that I have compassion. Recognize my capability for remorse. God Bless Amurycka Profunda – Love It or Leave It! I was so sad on the day that the Twin Towers fell. That's 2,600 less people on the Blue Green Planet that could have watched me on the Cibo Channel. But there's no time to be wasted in crying over entrepreneurial opportunities lost due to senseless death and destruction. If I hadn't learned as a child how to shut my heart like a steel trap – I wouldn't be here now making the best cookies in the cosmos! I was so happy on the day that I sent Mrs. Elysian-Phields, the Cookie Czarina, hurtling out into space strapped onto a nuclear warhead!"

..... Suddenly Gothra was wide-awake, horny and missing sex. She ran out into her Beef Jerky Mill garden, pulled down her pants and sat bare-assed on a rotten pumpkin. *"Mmm ..... this is sensual"* she murmured to herself, stretching out her arms and legs and giving into the pleasure. Then Gothra was seized by a joyful moment of creative inspiration ..... "I'll manufacture pumpkin toilets. They'll be made of glazed orange porcelain – along with imprints of sinister pumpkin smiles embedded into the tops of the seats. I'll make a deal with the Glade Plug-Ins people in the process – I'll definitely get them on board! Underpaid Third-World workers will earn next to nothing making them! With the profits derived from this project – I'll buy P. S. 1 in Long Guile-Land City, Queers, Nueva Jork – get rid of all the art inside it that's incomprehensible to the masses – and convert the place into a luxurious loft-palace for my daughter Elysia!"

This new business plan had made Gothra so exhilarated that she needed to cool off. To lessen the effects of the werewoolf blood that ran through her veins – she had started meditating. She sat herself back down on that rotten pumpkin, assumed the lotus position, closed her eyes, focused on her breathing and repeated the following mantras ..... *I believe in the power of orange ..... its essential nature mystifies Western man ..... let's face it a white man dressed in orange or yellow looks laughable ..... Maya Hiyuh Powuh will support me in my struggle to stop demonizing sex. I am now one with the 7th chakra, the Crown of Creation, infinite awareness and the violet spirituality of the Third-Eye Mind. This is heart-centered work that flows through the xylem and phloem of my being .....*

Gothra had finally learned how to get out of her own way and to just be. Her destiny had been revealed to her. From that moment forward, she would be spending eternity in a snowy biosphere where it was always Christmas.

THE PREISZCZ IS WREIGHT

THE PREISZCZ IS WREIGHT

DIOCLETIA MC-SASSFRAS, COME ON DOWN! JAMBALAYA SAINT-SHOEMAKER, COME ON DOWN! AVANT-GUARDIA POMPADOUR, COME ON DOWN! OLIGARCHIA OLIVEBRANCH, COME ON DOWN!

TELEPORTIA TUMBLEWEED, COME ON DOWN! CONCORDIA CRIPPLECRIK, COME ON DOWN! BACKSTABIA BLOODBEAST, COME ON DOWN! BOTOXIA BUBBLEBUTT, COME ON DOWN!

CHILLA-CHELLIA CHIPPENDALE, COME ON DOWN! ARSONIA KRYPTOWITCH, COME ON DOWN! FATALISTIKA FEATHERWEIGHT, COME ON DOWN! FORTUNOPOLIS FILAGREE, COME ON DOWN!

REALISIMUS RIPPLERUNE, COME ON DOWN! SEPTICIMIA CILANTROWICZ, COME ON DOWN!

MISSILECRISIA MILLSTONE, COME ON DOWN! ALTRUISTIKA TRUANCY, COME ON DOWN!

TEMPTONIUS TASERTICKLE, COME ON DOWN! TESTOSTERONIA TECTONICISER, COME ON DOWN! PHANTASMIA FALLACY, COME ON DOWN! LABYRINTHIA LIPOSUCK, COME ON DOWN!

KOLGATIA KOOLWHIP, COME ON DOWN! GASTRONOMIA GARGANTUA, COME ON DOWN! DEMYSTIFIA DOLOMITE, COME ON DOWN! TIPARILLIO TANTALUS, COME ON DOWN! AQUAVELVEETA NOXEMIUS, COME ON DOWN!

PARSIMONIUS PATRIA, COME ON DOWN! DEMONIO ÜBERMENSCH, COME ON DOWN! DIAPHANOUS DAIQUIRI, COME ON DOWN! MAGNANIMA MISTLETOE, COME ON DOWN! GARMONBOZIA GALAPAGOS, COME ON DOWN!

APOCRYPHA PASSAFIRE, COME ON DOWN! AGRIPPA PORCINIUS, COME ON DOWN! INFLUENZA MALARIUS, COME ON DOWN! AIDA SIDAPOLIS, COME ON DOWN! PANDEMIC APOCALYPSE, COME ON DOWN!

ABOUT THE AUTHOR

Writer / artist / performer Steve Bird is the author of "Catastrophically Consequential" (Hysterical Dementia, 2012) & "Hideous Exuberance" (published in a previous form by Vox Pop, 2009). Credits: Readings from "Catastrophically Consequential" at 292 East Third Street Gallery (NYC); Readings from "Hideous Exuberance" at Notes from Underground (Von Bar, NYC) & We'll Never Have Paris (107 Suffolk Street, NYC); Producer for the one-man / variety shows Sarcastic Passion, Smirk, Ass of Satan, Superfluous Disgruntlement & Hysterical Dementia; Appearances at / in conjunction with the New York International Fringe Festival, P. S. 122, Bowery Poetry Club, Under St. Marks & Collective Unconscious (Ludlow Street). Mr. Bird is a graduate of the Gallatin School of New York University.

Made in the USA
Charleston, SC
03 March 2013